FATAL FIXER UPPER

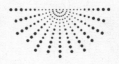

MAGGIE SHAYNE

0 9 8 7 6 5 4 3 2 1

❀ Created with Vellum

CHAPTER ONE

*J*n the time it took Kiley Brigham to submerge her head, rinse out the shampoo and sit up again, the temperature in the bathroom had plummeted from "steamy sauna" to somewhere around "clutch your arms and shiver." Sitting up straighter with rivulets fleeing her skin for warmer climes, sprouting goose bumps, she muttered, "Well, what the hell is *this?*" and then frowned harder because she could see her breath when she spoke.

Had Halloween week in Burnt Hills, New York turned suddenly, bitterly cold? There hadn't been any warning on the weather report. And even if there had been a sudden cold snap, the furnace should have kicked on. According to the overall-wearing, toolbox-carrying guy she'd hired to inspect the hundred-year-old house before agreeing to buy it, the heating system was in great shape. True, she hadn't run it much in the three days since she'd moved in, but it had kicked on once or twice when the mercury had dipped outside. It had been working fine.

She tilted her head, listening for the telltale rattle of hot water being forced through aging radiators, but she heard nothing. The furnace wasn't running.

Sighing, she rose from the water, stepped over the side of the tub onto the plush powder-blue bath mat, and reached for the matching towel. Her new shell-pink-and-white ceramic tiles might look great, but they definitely added to the chill, she decided, peering at the completely fogged-up mirror and then scurrying quickly through the door and into her bedroom for the biggest, warmest robe she could find.

As soon as she stepped into the bedroom, the chill was gone. She stood there wondering what the hell to make of that. Leaning back through the bathroom door, she felt that iciness hanging in the air. It was like stepping into a meat cooler. Leaning back out into the bedroom, she felt the same cozy warmth she always felt there.

Kiley shrugged, pulled the bathroom door closed and battled a delayed-reaction shiver. She closed her eyes briefly, just to tamp down the notion that the shiver was caused by something beyond the temperature, then turned to face her bedroom with its hardwood wainscoting so dark it looked like ebony, its crown molding the same, its freshly applied antique ivory paint in between. Her bedroom suite came close to matching: deep black cherry wood that bore the barest hint of blood red. The bedding and curtains in the tall, narrow windows were the color of French cream, as were the throw rugs on the dark hardwood floor. Ebony and ivory had been her notion for this room, and it worked.

"I love my new house," she said aloud, even as she sent a troubled glance back toward the bathroom. "And I'm going to stop looking for deep, dark secrets to explain the bargain-basement asking price. So, my bathroom has a draft. So what?"

Nodding in resolve, she moved to the closet, opened the door, then paused, staring. One of the dresses was moving, the hanger rocking back and forth mere millimeters, as if someone had jostled it.

Only, no one had.

She could have kicked herself for the little shiver that ran up her spine. She didn't even believe in the sorts of things that were whispering through her brain and had been ever since she'd moved in.

I jerked open the door, it caused air-movement, the dress moved a little. No big deal.

In spite of her internal scolding, her eyes felt wider than she would have liked as she perused the closet's interior. Her handy-man-slash-house-inspector had asked if she'd like a light installed in there. She'd said no. Now she was thinking about calling him tomorrow morning to change her answer. Meanwhile, she spotted her robe and snatched it off its hanger with the speed of a cobra snatching a fieldmouse. She back-stepped, slammed the closet door, and felt her heart start to pound in her chest.

Breathe, she thought. And then she did, a long, deep, slow inhale that filled her lungs to bursting, a brief delay while she counted to four, and a thorough, cleansing exhale that emptied her lungs entirely. She repeated it three times, got a grip on herself and then felt stupid.

She did *not* believe in closet-dwelling bogeymen. Hell, she'd made her career debunking nonsense like that. More precisely, putting phony psychics, gurus and ghost busters out of business in this spooky little tourist town. And nobody liked it. Not the town supervisor, the town council, the tourism bureau, and least of all, the phony psychics, gurus and ghost busters. But, thanks to the Constitution, freedom of the press couldn't be banned on the grounds that it was bad for business.

She pulled her bathrobe on, relishing the feel of plush fabric on her skin, and then took a breath of courage and turned to face the bathroom again. Her hairbrush was in there, along with her skin lotions, cuticle trimmer and toothbrush. And she still had to pull the plug and let the water run out of the bathtub. She was going back in. A cold draft was nothing to be afraid of.

Crossing the room, one foot in front of the other, she moved firmly to the bathroom door, closed her hand on its oval, antique porcelain doorknob, and opened it. The air that greeted her was no longer icy. In fact, it was as warm as the air in the bedroom.

She sighed in relief as she stepped into the room. But her relief died and the chill returned to her soul when she saw the mirror, no longer coated in fog, but something else. Something far, far worse.

Dripping bloody letters on the still-damp mirror spelled out "House of Death."

Someone screamed. It wasn't until she was down the stairs, out the door, and about fifteen yards up the heaving, cracked sidewalk that Kiley realized the scream had been her own.

She stood there in the dead of night, barefoot, clutching her robe against the whipping October wind and staring back at her dream house with its turrets and gables and its widow's walk up top. Such a beautiful place, old and solid. And framed right now by the scarlet and shimmering yellow of sugar maples and poplar trees at the peak of their fall color. Swallowing hard, she lowered her gaze, focusing on her car in the driveway beside the house. Leaping Lana was a four-door sedan in rust-brown that ate gas like M&Ms and sounded like a tank.

Kiley squared her shoulders and forced herself to march over there even though it meant moving *toward* her house when every cell in her body was itching to move *away* from it instead. She opened Lana's door and climbed in. She couldn't quite keep herself from checking the back seat first. It was clear. The keys were in the switch, because if someone was brave enough to steal Kiley Brigham's car, she'd always thought she would enjoy the vengeance she'd be forced to wreak on their pathetic asses, and besides, who would steal Lana, anyway?

She turned the key. Lana growled in protest at being bothered at such an ungodly hour, but finally came around and cooperatively backed her boat-size backside out into the street. As Kiley shifted into Drive, she glanced up at her house again.

There was someone standing in her bedroom window looking back at her.

And then there wasn't. She squinted, rubbed her eyes. The image hadn't moved, hadn't turned away. The dark silhouette she knew she had seen simply vanished. Faded. Like mist.

"Okay, screw this," she muttered, and she stomped on Lana's pedal and didn't let off until they'd reached the offices of the *Burnt Hills Gazette.* Her tiny office there held three things Kiley dearly needed just then: a change of clothes, a telephone, and a drink.

She was so together by the time the police arrived that they actually seemed skeptical. At least until they headed back to her recently acquired house and saw the message on the mirror for themselves. Kiley preferred to stay out in the bedroom—and even that gave her the creeps—while the cops clustered around her bathroom sink debating whether the substance on her mirror was blood. One opined that it looked like paint, and another said it was cherry syrup. At that point the conversation turned to previous cases where what was thought to be blood turned out to be something else entirely, like corn syrup with red food coloring added— a tale that the officers found laugh-worthy.

She interrupted their fun by standing as close to her bathroom door as she wanted to get, and clearing her throat. The laughter stopped, the cops looked up.

"Excuse me, but shouldn't one of you be taking a sample of that? And maybe checking my house for signs of forced entry?"

"Did that, ma'am," one cop said, sending a long-suffering look toward another. "No signs of a break-in. You sure the place was locked?"

"Of course I'm sure the place was..." She stopped, pursed her lips, thought it over with brutal honesty. "Actually, I forget to lock up as often as I remember."

"Well, at least you're aware this was the work of an intruder."

She frowned at him. "Well, of course it was an intruder. What else could it have been?"

"You know how folks get around here. Half the time we get a call like this, the homeowner insists some kind of ghost was responsible."

"Especially at this time of year," another cop said, and they all nodded or rolled their eyes with "isn't that ridiculous" looks at one another.

"I don't believe in ghosts," she managed to say, rubbing her arms against the chill that came from within. "As to how the intruder got in. I'm not even sure it's all that important. The fact is that he did get in. And I know that because I saw him."

"You saw him? Excellent." Cop number one—his name tag read Hanlon—pulled out a notepad and pen. "Okay, where and when did you see the intruder?"

"He was standing right there in the window, looking down at me when I backed the car out."

"So, you didn't see anyone while you were inside. Only after you'd left?"

"Right."

"And can you describe him?"

She recalled the misty silhouette behind the veil of her curtains. "Uh, no."

"But you're sure it was a male," Hanlon said.

She narrowed her eyes and searched her memory. "No. No, I can't even be sure of that much. It was dark. It was just a shadow, a dark silhouette in the window." She sighed in frustration. "Has there been a rash of break-ins that I should know about, anything like this at all?" she asked, almost hoping the answer would be yes.

Hanlon shook his head. "We've got hardly any crime around

here, Ms. Brigham. Little enough that you'd be reading about it if there had been anything like that."

She nodded. "We're so hungry for stories we've been covering the missing prostitutes from Albany."

"You work for the press?" he asked.

"Yeah. *Burnt Hills Gazette.*" More people came in. They carried cases and headed for her bathroom. She watched them, her gaze unfocused. One swabbed a sample of the stuff from the mirror, dropped it into a vial and capped it. Another snapped photos. A third started coating her pretty shell-pink-and-white bathroom tiles in what looked like fireplace soot in search of fingerprints.

The guy with the swabs took out an aerosol can of something —the label read Luminol—and sprayed it at the mirror, then he turned off the lights.

Kiley sucked in a breath when the grisly message glowed blue in the darkness.

"It's blood, all right," the guy said, flipping the light back on.

Officer Hanlon moved up beside Kiley and put a hand on her shoulder as if he thought she might be close to losing it. "We'd probably better start thinking about who your enemies are, Ms. Brigham."

She swallowed hard. "It would be easier to tell you who they aren't, and it would make a way shorter list." The cop frowned. Another one nodded, coming out of the bathroom. "That's probably true."

Hanlon sent him a questioning look and he went on. "She's the chick who writes those columns discrediting all the mumbo-jumbo types in town."

"Aah, right. Kiley Brigham. It didn't click at first." Hanlon eyed her. "Is this the first death threat you've received, Ms. Brigham?"

"You think that's what it is? A threat?"

He shrugged. "Reads that way to me."

Kiley sighed. "Yeah, it would be my first."

"Wow." His brows arched high, as if he was surprised she didn't get threatened on a daily basis.

"Look, I'm not a demon here. I don't eat babies or kick puppies. I just tell the truth." She shrugged. "Can I help it if that makes the liars of the world angry?"

"Can you think of anyone in particular who could have taken their anger this far?"

"Yeah, I can think of several. Most of them hold public office, though."

Hanlon looked alarmed by that. "I hope you're kidding."

"Maybe. Half. So, what should I do?"

"Get yourself a security system," the officer said. "Something that's not going to let you get away with forgetting to lock up. In the meantime, is there someone who could stay with you tonight? A friend, relative, someone like that?"

The question made her stomach ache, though she didn't know why. It wasn't as if she gave a damn that she didn't have any friends or family, that she was, in fact, utterly alone in the world. She could care less. Hell, if friends were what she wanted, she'd be out making them, instead of pissing off as many people as possible on a weekly basis. Screw friends.

"Ma'am?"

She shrugged. "I'll spend the night at my office. There's security there. Tomorrow I'll see about getting a system installed here. Thanks for coming out."

He nodded. "We'll be another hour here," he told her. "You can go, if you want. We'll lock up when we leave."

"Yeah, like *that's* gonna do any good," she muttered as she headed out of the room. And then she stopped in the hallway and wondered just what the hell she had meant by that. She shook it off, told herself it didn't matter.

She had a major day tomorrow. *Major.*

Tomorrow she was going to bust the one New Age fraud who had eluded her ever since she'd begun her weekly series. She'd planned for this, prepared for it, set up an elaborate scheme to make it happen. And nothing as mundane as a death threat written in blood on her bathroom mirror while she was standing a few feet away wearing nothing but a towel was going to stop her from seeing it through.

CHAPTER TWO

*W*hen *she* was around, the hair on the back of his neck bristled the way a cat's does in the presence of a killer dog. He always tensed up the instant before he saw her. It was *not* a case of extrasensory perception, no matter what his harebrained assistant might like to believe. More likely a case of instinctive self-preservation.

She was nearby, all right. It wasn't a scent, exactly, though now that he was alert, he could just detect a faint whiff of that aroma that always floated around her. Not a powerful fragrance —not even a perfume or cologne. Maybe it was the soap she used or something. He only knew it was unique, an aroma he equated with his biggest headache. It shouldn't seem like a sexy scent to him. But it did.

Jack lifted his head and scanned the dim room, but he couldn't see her. Candles flickered from the shelves that lined the walls. Their dancing light was refracted in the slow-turning crystal prisms suspended from the ceiling and transformed into living rainbows that crept over the walls and floor. The purple curtains that separated this room from the rest of the shop were closed, and revealed nothing.

She was out there, though. No doubt about it. The persistent little pain in the ass.

Finally, Jack refocused on the nervous woman who sat across from him, fidgeting with her purse straps. Really on edge, this one. Even more than most people were their first time. At least he knew why; she was just another weapon in Kiley Brigham's one-woman crusade against charlatans like him.

He barely restrained himself from cussing loud and long—not a good quality in one who purported to be in touch with the spirit world—and forced a serene smile for his new client.

"I'm sorry, Martha. I just can't seem to get a response from your dear departed husband."

"You can't?"

He shook his head sadly. "It's odd. Feels almost as if he doesn't exist." Jack pinned her with his gaze. "As if you made him up, just to, I don't know, test me or something."

She blinked twice, gaping, and Jack saw just enough guilt in her eyes to confirm his guess.

"That's impossible, of course," he went on. "You wouldn't do something like that, would you, Martha?"

"Of course not!"

"Maybe you'll have better luck with another medium. I could give you some names."

"No, thank you. I'll just..." She let her voice trail off as she rose. Her small wooden chair scraped over the marble tiles, a growl of discord breaking the spell of the haunting New Age music that whispered in magical Gaelic of fairies and poisoned glens.

"Don't rush off," Jack told her, rising as well. "I insist on refunding your money. I'm not a thief, you know."

She took a step backward, toward the curtain, clearly itching to get out of there. She actually leaned toward the curtain as she moved, actually reached behind her for it long before she was close enough to touch it. "You, uh, you can mail it to me," she rushed on, her feet shuffling away from him, slowly but steadily.

"All right. I'll do that. Do you want to give me your address, Martha, or shall I just save time and send it to Kiley Brigham?"

The purple curtain flew open even as Martha kept groping for it, and he was not surprised to see Kiley herself on the other side, mad as hell, judging by the way her face was screwed up.

"Damn you to hell, McCain!" Her hands were braced on her hips and she was breathing a little too fast. She did the heaving-bosom thing well. She certainly had the bosoms for it. Candle-light illuminated the pink spots on her cheeks and the fire in her green eyes. Cat's eyes, she had, and hair blacker than ink. Hell, she ought to be the one running this scam. Her looks would attract customers like moths to the porch light.

Well, she'd have to dress the part, of course. Those tight-fitting, faded jeans and that T-shirt that read "Keep Your Opinions Out of My Uterus" would never cut it.

But Kiley Brigham, girl columnist, wasn't interested in taking up his line of work. Instead, she was intent on ruining what he'd built into a lucrative business.

Martha, he realized, was long gone. Must have darted out of the room while he'd been perusing his nemesis, who, he realized, had been perusing him right back.

"Tell me something, Brigham," he said, sitting back down in his chair. "Were you mauled by a pack of mediums as a child?"

She sent him a smirk that should have burned holes through him, but said nothing. Then her probing green eyes got busy scanning the room: narrow, suspicious, searching. He hated to admit it made him a little nervous to have her looking around his place so closely.

"So, what do you want?" he asked to break her concentration. "You come for a reading? Want me to tell your future, Brigham? Read your palm? What?"

As planned, her gaze returned to him. "How the hell did you know I was here?"

He rolled his eyes. "I'm *clairvoyant*, remember?"

"And I'm a Republican."

A grin tugged at the corners of his lips. He battled it and finally won. "So, what do I have to do? Slap you with a restraining order?"

"You really think it would help?"

"Couldn't hurt," he said.

She bristled, but only for a moment. It seemed to him the wind left her sails far more quickly than usual. She heaved a sigh and sank into the chair the other woman had occupied. "Did you have to scare her like that, McCain? You know how tough it is to find out-of-work actresses who come as cheap as that one?"

He did smile then. It seemed safe. Her rage was ebbing, and in record time. It made him wonder what was wrong. "You want something to drink?"

"Not if you're gonna try to foist some herbal, trance-inducing tea on me, I don't."

"Guess you're outta luck, then."

She rolled her eyes. "You don't really drink that crap. You can fool everyone else in this town, especially the tourists, but you can't fool me. Why don't you drop the act?"

He pretended to think it over, then said, "Nah. Business is booming these days." He leaned forward, flattening his palms to the table. "Largely thanks to that nasty little column of yours discrediting my competitors one by one on a weekly basis."

She leaned over the table, too, her palms on the gleaming hardwood surface like his, her face only inches away. "You make a living by feeding innocent victims a line of bull. They hand over their hard-earned money for the privilege of being duped."

"I make a living by giving people psychologically sound advice. People who might not listen to a therapist. I'm good at what I do. I help people. You, on the other hand, make a living putting hard-working people like me out of business. I'll take my karma over yours anytime."

"Karma, schmarma." She sat back, her palms gliding across the small table. "You know as well as I do that there's no such thing. No psychics, no ghosts, no magic."

"No God?" He asked the question idly, as if he couldn't care less about her answer.

She was silent for a long moment, so preoccupied she didn't even notice him looking at her. Her eyes were a little puffy, as if she hadn't slept. There was a tightness to her face that suggested worry.

Then, her gaze still focused inward, she said, "I don't get it, McCain."

"Don't get what?"

"Look at this picture. It's skewed, don't you think? You're the crook. I'm the crusader. So, how come you get the adulation and I get the hate mail?"

"It's adulation you want, huh? The love of your fellow man?"

"I don't want anyone to love me. I've scraped by without it for this long, haven't I?" She said it lightly, rushing on before he could identify the emotion that had crossed her face. "I'd be happy if they'd just stop with the death threats."

Jack started to laugh, but it died in his throat when he looked into her eyes. There had been no lightness in her tone on those words, no laughter in her eyes. She wasn't kidding. "You've been getting death threats?"

"Just the one. You wouldn't happen to know anything about it, would you? Quaint little love note on my bathroom mirror, written in what the police department tells me is blood. Human blood, I learned this morning. Cute, huh?"

It wasn't his imagination. She shivered when she said it, though the way she clenched her jaw made it obvious she was trying real hard not to show the slightest hint of upset. It was as he was studying the pallor of her skin that Jack noticed his own new position. Just when the hell had he come out of his chair and around to her side of the table? She rose as he stared down at her, as if she didn't like having to look up at him. Or maybe it was that she didn't want him to see her teetering.

Too late for that, though.

"When did this happen?"

She shrugged, avoiding his eyes. "I was soaking in the tub last night. I got up and went into the bedroom for my robe, and when I came back it was there on the bathroom mirror. For all I know they could have been right on the other side of the shower curtain from me at some point." Her lower lip quivered, but she bit it hard and quick, then gave her head a shake. "Bastard's lucky I didn't see him."

"This isn't funny, Kiley. God. You said the police are on this?"

She nodded. "Look, don't trouble yourself over it. I didn't come here for sympathy."

He wanted the animosity back. He wanted to fight with her, wanted her back to insulting his moral fiber instead of making him feel sick on her behalf. "No, you just dropped in to chat, ruin my business and accuse me of threatening your life. I love these little visits of yours." As an attempt to rekindle the banter, it was sadly lacking. But it worked all the same.

"Drop dead, McCain."

Ah, that was more like it. "Same to you, Brigham."

Her head came up fast, green eyes meeting his, wider than he'd ever seen them. "You mean that?"

He felt as if she'd punched him in the gut. But she just stood there, waiting for an answer, probing his eyes and looking madder than hell, capable of murder and as vulnerable as a wet cat all at the same time. His hands moved up to grasp her shoulders. "I didn't leave you any death threat, Brigham. Whenever I get the urge to tell you to drop dead, I say it right to your pretty face. And if I'd been lurking on the other side of the curtain while you were soaking in the tub, the worst thing I'd have done is cop a peek. And I think you know it."

She blinked, swallowed audibly and nodded. "I didn't really figure a message in blood was your style."

"Because I'm such a swell guy?"

She smirked, a little of the old mischief backlighting the fear in her eyes. "Because you know me well enough to know I'd kick your ass if I ever found out."

"Any time you wanna try, Brigham."

No comeback. Hell, he couldn't remember the last time he'd sparred with her and she'd run out of trash talk. It made him uncomfortable to know just how upset she must be to let it affect her acid tongue. And he had to change the subject, before he started getting some stupid urge to help her out, somehow.

He cleared his throat, realized his hands were still on her shoulders, and lowered them to his sides while searching his brain for a safer topic. "So, uh, how did you manage to get in? How did Chris not notice you lurking outside the curtain?"

"You mean the scrawny kid with the quartz earring and the bright yellow dust mop on his head?"

"That's his hair."

"No shit?" She shrugged. "Anyway, he was busy humming along with whatever flaky-ass music you have playing out there."

"You know, if you could manage to stop being so damned *pleasant* all the time, you might attract friendlier fans." He felt his lips thin as he tried to find a way to give her some free advice without imparting the impression that he actually gave a damn. "And you might try being a little less controversial, while you're at it."

"And how would you suggest I do that, McCain? You want me to put in for a personality transplant?"

"Maybe try toning down your columns for a while. Find a new subject for a few weeks, give this a chance to blow over."

"Yeah, you'd like that, wouldn't you?

She went on a rant about freedom of the press and the First Amendment, but he wasn't really hearing her. He was noticing the way her fingers trembled as she pushed a stray lock of hair behind her ear. And then he noticed how the candles still flickering in the reading room—you had to set the scene—filled her eyes with amber glow and highlighted her hair in raven-blue.

"I will never stop now," she concluded. "If I stop, they win."

He nodded thoughtfully, as if he'd heard every angry word. "On second thought, maybe the personality transplant wouldn't be a bad idea after all."

She hauled her backpack onto her shoulder. "I gotta go."

"I'll walk you out." He walked her through the shop to the front door.

She looked around his shop, those witch's eyes of hers searching for secrets, tricks. She wouldn't find any. Jack's tricks were all in the minds of his customers. This crap was real to them.

Brigham stopped at the front door, turning to face him. For a very brief moment he had the feeling she didn't want to leave any more than he wanted her to. Damn. He must be overworked or something. They couldn't stand each other. They *detested* each other. If someone had asked him to name his number-one enemy, he'd have named her without batting an eye. And he had no doubt she would name him if asked the same question. He had about as much clairvoyance as her ancient, smoke-belching car and she knew it. He reveled in rubbing her nose in her inability to get the goods on him, and it drove her nuts!

It was strange, the relationship they'd developed over the past few years. She, always trying to trip him up. He, always struggling to stay a half-step ahead of her. It was an ongoing contest with no clear winner in sight. He'd grown kind of used to it...maybe was even *enjoyed* her irritating persistence in some twisted way.

Nah.

He looked down at her and then he flinched at the size of the knot that formed in his stomach. For a second, he'd seen it in her face, just as plain as day: cold, dark fear. She hid it quickly, covering it up with the stubborn determination he was used to seeing there. But not fast enough. Not before he'd spotted it haunting her emerald eyes. It wasn't an emotion he'd ever seen there before. She was probably the gutsiest loudmouth he'd ever known.

She cleared her throat, reached for the door handle. "Well..."

"Yeah."

She nodded once, stepped outside into the normal world again. He winced inwardly, because he had the feeling someone was about to drop a piano on her.

He caught the door before it could swing closed. "Brigham?"

"What?"

"Watch your back, okay?"

"You bet your amethysts, I will." She winked, then strode away as if she wasn't terrified of being alone.

CHAPTER THREE

*J*ack McCain might be the lowest form of pond slime, Kiley thought as she sat at her desk back in her office at the *Burnt Hills Gazette*, staring at her empty computer screen. But he wasn't the kind of guy who would leave messages in human blood on a bathroom mirror.

She'd known that before she'd asked him, but hadn't been able to resist asking all the same, just to gauge his reaction.

There was a tap on her office door before it opened, and her boss, the most gorgeous woman in town if Kiley was any judge, stepped inside. "Did you get anything on McCain?"

Sighing, Kiley shook her head. "He knew it was a setup. Smelled it like a rat smells cheese."

Barbara Benedict laughed and raked a hand through her pixie-cut ash-blond hair. "You ever wonder about that, Kiley?"

"About what? Whether he's part rat?"

"Whether he...maybe really *has* something. Some kind of...you know."

"God, it would be one warped Universe if it handed out gifts like that to guys like Jack McCain."

"Yeah, he's already got the looks, the charm—you're right, it would be unfair."

Kiley hadn't been referring to Jack's looks or his charm, but she didn't bother to correct her employer.

"So, did you ask him about the, uh—the incident?"

"Uh-huh."

"And?"

"Oh, hell, you should have seen it. It was the performance of a lifetime, Barb. The hint of worry in his eyes. The concerned knit in his brow. The hand on my shoulder. It was perfect. He almost had me believing he was worried about me."

"You don't really think he *did* it, though."

Kiley lowered her head. "No, it's not his style."

"Then why are you so sure his concern is phony?"

"Because Jack McCain doesn't worry about anybody or anything besides himself and his bank balance. If he's concerned at all, it's that I'll try to pin this on him and disrupt his livelihood in the process. No, Jack is a con man. I've dealt with men like him before. I know 'em when I see 'em."

Barbara tipped her head to one side. "You talking about your ex now?"

"They're so much alike it's tough not to compare."

"What did that guy *do* to you, anyway? You haven't talked about it since you moved out here. I'm dying of curiosity."

Kiley pushed her hair behind one ear, rising from her chair and grabbing her shoulder bag from the desk. "I gotta go find a subject for this week's column. I've got a bear for an editor and she'll skin me alive if I don't." She sent Barbara a wink, then moved past her and out of the office.

Kiley walked out through the parking lot, trying to let the slanting October sunshine lift her spirits. She inhaled the scent of dying leaves, tasted late autumn in the air, told herself the alarm system would be all installed by the time she went to bed and that all was right with the world. But it wasn't easy to shake off the chill that had settled into her bones since she'd seen that message in the mirror.

At her car, she ran a hand over its sun-warmed fender. "You up for a ride, Lana?"

The car sat there, silent, ready. Her trusty steed. It was way better than the Porsche she used to drive. Lana had *character*. She unlocked the driver's door, checked the back seat and got in. Then she drove into town to have her lunch in the park, as she did every day, weather permitting. People knew where to find her. She used to consider that a good thing.

Now, though, maybe not so much.

Still, she needed a tip, and this was her best shot at landing one. She walked to the corner hot dog stand. "Hey, Bernie. Gimme the usual."

Smiling, the compact, muscular vendor began putting her foot-long-with-the-works together. "Heard you had a break-in last night," he said as he heaped on the sauerkraut.

Her brows rose. "Where'd you hear that?"

"Around."

Bernie's son was on the town's police force. But she wouldn't rat him out for spreading gossip. It was a small town. Everybody knew everybody's business.

"You okay?"

"Yeah. Got a whole new security system being installed tonight."

"Smart." He put her dog in a cardboard boat, set it aside and fished an icy diet cola from his cooler. "Three ninety-five, same as always."

She slid a five-dollar bill across the top of his shiny stand. "Keep the change, same as always." She took her dog and drink and started to turn away.

"So, you sure it was someone that broke in, not someone who was already there?"

She turned back to face the hot dog vendor again. "What do you mean, Bernie? There was no one there but me."

"Well, yeah, but you know the stories about that place. It has a history."

She blinked three times as every part of her went on high alert. "What kind of a history?"

His face changed; he looked suddenly...different. Worried, and maybe regretting his words. "I, uh—I figured you knew. Then again, it's old stuff. You've only been in town a year."

"Two years," she corrected him. "And I've only been in the house for a few days. So, if there's something I should know, then I'd appreciate you telling me."

He grinned at her suddenly and waved a hand. "I'm just picking on you, kid. You know this town, it's full of ghost stories."

"My house has ghost stories?"

"I told you, I was kidding. Go on, get outta here."

She wasn't going to get anything out of Bernie. Not that she thought a ghost had anything to do with what had happened in her bathroom. Even if her stomach did tighten up at the word, and even if it was the same theory her imagination kept posing. Still, if there were things she hadn't known about the place, things the real estate folks had failed to disclose, they were liable to find themselves the next topic of one of her columns.

She walked to her favorite bench, the one near the fountain, sat down and proceeded to share scraps of hot dog bun with the pigeons while she opened a notebook and wrote a note to herself to do some research on her house.

Someone sat down right beside her, and she knew just by the way her skin prickled who it was. Without looking up, she said, "Hello, McCain. What, you didn't get enough of me this morning?"

"Don't be nasty, Brigham. I come bearing gifts."

She finally looked up at him. He had a foot-long hot dog with the works, and a diet cola. She said, "You're going to give me your lunch?"

"You already have one. Or are you telling me you could eat two of these pups?"

"I could eat three and still have room for dessert."

He smiled. "I like a woman with an appetite."

"*You* like a woman with a pulse."

"Well, yeah. A pulse is good, too." He leaned back on the bench and took a big bite of the hot dog, giving her the perfect opportunity to do the same. God, she loved them. Probably unhealthy as all hell, but so worth it.

He washed his bite down with a gulp of the cola. "I felt sorry for getting the best of you yet again this morning."

"Oh, I'm sure."

"Hated leaving you without a column this week."

"Mmm-hmm." She kept eating, pretending to be only barely listening, but in truth, she was rapt. Was her arch rival going to give her a tip? It sure seemed to be what he was getting around to.

"Anyway, frauds who cause more harm than good need to be shut down. I'm as onboard with that as you are."

"Then how do you sleep at night?"

"You wanna shut up and listen, or should I take my information and go home?"

She faced him, a serene smile on her lips, batting her eyes in mock innocence.

He rolled his in response, then brought his napkin to the corner of her mouth to dab something away. Ketchup or relish, she guessed. "There's a new player in town. He's rented out that little brick box on Main and Oak that's been vacant for so long."

"The one that used to be the barber shop?"

He nodded.

"So, what's his game?"

"He starts out small. Tells people he had a dream about them, and that he has information for them. Then he gives them some cock-and-bull story about staying out of traffic on a certain day, and asks them to make an appointment for a more in-depth session. That first bit is free, but when they come back he starts really soaking them."

"How badly?"

"Fifty bucks for the first session. Which isn't bad, but then the upsells start. There are all these charms and talismans they have to buy in order to avoid disaster, and those start at a hundred and go up to three. He's calling these people at home, claiming to have urgent messages that they need to hear, convincing them to come back for another fifty-dollar session. It's all older folks. One of my regulars said her mother had laid out more than a thousand dollars in the past month. The guy's ruthless."

"The guy's a bastard." She nodded. "Okay, I'll get on it. Thanks for the tip."

He smiled. "Can't have people like him giving us legitimate psychic counselors a bad name."

"You're as legitimate as this hot dog is health food, McCain."

"Hey, if I were a fake, you'd have had me by now. You're too good not to."

"Yeah, and flattery will win me right over."

He shrugged. "Have it your way." He got to his feet, popped the last bite of his hot dog into his mouth.

"McCain?"

Still chewing, he looked at her.

"You know anything about my house?"

He swallowed, swiped his mouth with the napkin. "Like what?"

"I don't know. I heard it had a history."

His brows rose. "What kind of history?"

"I got the feeling it was the kind that was right up your alley."

"You mean it's haunted?" He covered the stunned expression

he wore with a grin. "Hell, I didn't think you believed in any of that stuff, Brigham."

"Oh, I haven't given up on the possibility. Just my faith in my fellow humans, and in my chances of ever finding proof that there's... something more." She watched his face, because frankly, she had trouble swallowing that *he* really believed in the nonsense he was selling.

He swallowed hard. "Tell you the truth, Brigham, I only came to this town about six months before you did. I wouldn't know much of its history."

"I figured you probably would have mentioned it if you had."

"You're not thinking your break-in and death threat were the actions of some kind of ghost or demon or something, are you? Because that kind of thinking could make you careless. It could get you killed."

She thought about how icy cold it had become in the bathroom just before the message had appeared on her mirror. She thought about the clothes moving in the closet and the shadowy shape in her window. She almost told him about all of that. But then she bit her lip and shook her head. "Nah. I don't think any such thing. See you later, McCain."

"Yeah. See you."

Kiley watched him walk away as she finished her hot dog and her cola. Then she headed to the library and asked for help from the librarian. The woman promptly produced a book titled *The Haunted History of Burnt Hills*. It was a local author, self-published, but exactly what she needed.

She took the volume with her when she went to stake out the little brick building on the corner of Main and Oak Streets.

CHAPTER FOUR

$\mathcal{J}$ ack sat in his teenage employee's rusted-out pickup truck around the corner from where Kiley Brigham's car was parked. She wasn't in it, not just then, anyway. She'd sat there for a long time with the overhead light on, reading something. Then, when Randeaux de Loup, as he called himself, had left his little brick shop, she'd gone over there.

"You think she's going to break in?" Chris asked, pushing his mop of yellow hair off his brown forehead.

"I imagine she's going through the garbage."

"Why do you think that?"

"Because it's what I would do. Scoot over to her car, Chris, and see if you can get a look at what she's been reading."

Chris sent Jack a scared look. Sighing, Jack pulled a twenty out of his pocket and handed it to him. He snatched it and was out of the car a heartbeat later. The kid kept to the shadows, crouching low as he ran. Moments later he was back, getting into his pickup and handing Jack a book.

"Jeeze, I said see what it was, not steal it!"

"Oh. Uh. Sorry. You want me to put it back?"

Jack looked up, didn't see any sign of Kiley returning to her car. "In a minute." The book had a page folded over. He flipped it open to see what Kiley had been reading.

"Why are we following her, anyway?"

"To make sure no one murders her," he said.

"You like her. I *knew* it."

"I can't stand her. I just know damn well I'd be on top of the list of suspects if something should happen to the irritating little —hell, this is what I was afraid of."

"What?" Chris leaned over, trying to get a look at the pages Jack was reading.

Jack turned the book so he could see the black-and-white snapshot of the house, looking slightly newer.

"Hey, isn't that where Miss Brigham lives?"

"Yeah, and according to this, it's haunted."

"Well, yeah. Everybody knows that."

Jack just sat there staring at him in disbelief. "You knew she was living in a haunted house, and you didn't tell me?"

"Didn't know you'd be interested." He shrugged. "I thought you didn't believe in that stuff."

"I don't. But if you haven't learned another thing from me after all this time, Chris, you should have learned that it's not what *I* believe that matters." Something moved over by the brick building. Jack shoved the book back into Chris's hands. "Go put it back right where you found it. And don't let her see you."

"Right." Chris slid out of the vehicle again and managed to get the job done.

It was as he was heading back to the pickup that Jack heard a tap on his window and turned to see Brigham standing there, looking at him. Telling himself to think fast, he rolled the window down.

"You following me, McCain?"

"Saw your car. Thought I'd pull over for a sec. Just to watch your back."

"So, you're my bodyguard now?"

"You wish," he said. She rolled her eyes, but he kept speaking. "Find anything?"

"Client list," she said with a smile. "Jackpot."

"Yeah? What are you going to do with it?"

"You really wanna know? Buy the Sunday paper and find out with the rest of Burnt Hills." "That's gratitude for you. See if I ever give you another scoop."

"Hey, did I say I wasn't grateful?"

He shrugged, glanced around. "It's getting dark earlier, isn't it?"

"It's fall, Jack. That's what happens."

"You get your locks changed yet?"

She glanced at her watch. "Whole security system. The workers are probably still there. I really have to get home."

Something changed in her voice when she said that. He cleared his throat, told himself to shut the hell up, but the words came tumbling out, anyway. "You want me to come along? Just to...you know, take a look around?"

She fixed her eyes on him, brows pulling together as her head tipped slowly to one side. "You really *are* playing bodyguard, aren't you?"

He shrugged. "It's not a bad body. It'd be a shame if something happened to it."

"I didn't think you liked me, McCain."

"I never said I liked you, Brigham."

She smiled at him. "Actually, I *would* like you to come with me. There's something I want to talk to you about."

His throat went a little dry because he thought he knew what it was. And he'd walked right into it, hadn't he? "You wanna ride with me?" she asked.

"Sure." He glanced up, saw Chris frozen on the sidewalk, looking panicky. But Jack was certain Kiley hadn't seen the kid messing around near her car. He got out of the truck, waved at the kid.

"What's he doing wandering around?" Kiley asked.

"Had to take a leak," Jack said. "I'm riding with Ms. Brigham, kid. See you at the shop tomorrow."

Chris said something that emerged as an indecipherable squeak and hurried to his pickup, passing them on the sidewalk as they walked to Kiley's car. Jack smiled down at his nemesis. "We go for pie sometimes after work. I let him drive once in a while."

"That's nice of you."

He shrugged. As explanations went, it was full of holes, but he wasn't sure it mattered. He slid into the passenger side of her car. She got behind the wheel. "Lana, this is Jack. Jack, Lana."

Frowning, Jack swung his head around, half expecting to see someone in the back seat. But no one was there. "Uh, I'm not following."

"What, your car doesn't have a name?"

"Oh. The car. Right. Funny."

She shrugged, started the motor and drove them through the curving lanes of Burnt Hills, beneath a canopy of autumn colors, fallen leaves stirring on the roadsides as they passed.

"So, what is it you wanted to talk to me about?" Jack asked. "Finally ready to admit I'm the only legitimate psychic in town and call a truce?"

"Maybe I am."

He gaped in surprise. She only blinked at him, then glanced down at the book that lay on the seat in between them. "Have you read that book?"

He looked at it as if for the first time. "No."

"Well, according to it, my house has been considered one of the most haunted in Saratoga County for the past thirty years."

He closed his eyes. God, he'd had no idea it was that bad.

"I need a ghost buster. I need one that even I can't prove is a fraud. And the only one I've tried and tried to discredit, and failed to discredit...is you."

He swallowed the huge lump in his throat. This wasn't happening. It couldn't be happening.

"So," she went on, "I'm forced to admit the faint possibility that you *might* actually be legitimate. And even more weirdly, I feel I have to ask for your help."

"My... help?" It was happening.

She was turning the car into the driveway now. There was a white minivan parked there with Gates Security Systems painted on the side. The old house rose up before him like a guardian at the gate of a treasure, daring him to bring it on. He could almost hear it laughing, asking him, "Just what are you gonna do now, Slick?"

His mouth felt dry. He wished for something to drink.

"I know there's no love lost between the two of us, McCain. But do you think you could put that aside for a little while?"

He met her eyes, saw the hope in them, and the fear. "Yeah, I could do that. What do you want me to do?"

"Just come inside. Feel the place. See if you...pick up on anything."

He nodded, as if he'd be more than happy to help her out. But he'd already made up his mind what his diagnosis would be. He was *not* going to find any hint of any "presence" in Kiley Brigham's house. Not even if Casper himself performed an Irish jig in the living room. No way. Because if she thought there were ghosts in her house, she would ask him to get rid of them. And if she asked him to get rid of them, he would have to fake his way through it. Otherwise, she would have exactly what she had always wanted—proof that he was a fraud. So, it would all go better if he didn't find anything at all.

There wouldn't be anything to find, anyway. He was not a real ghost buster and there were no real ghosts. Problem solved.

"Lead the way."

"Thanks, Jack. I appreciate it."

He thought she really meant it. Guilt pricked his conscience.

She got out of the car, then waited for him to come around to her side before moving to the sidewalk and up to the front door. It stood open, the light from inside spilling out. Men in overalls were on the other side, mostly standing around, though one of them was twisting a screwdriver, tightening a box near the door.

"How's it going?" she asked, leading Jack inside, past the men.

The worker nodded. "Just fine. We're all finished." He straightened from his task, dropping the screwdriver into a loop on his belt. Then he pulled a fat envelope from his pocket and handed it to her. "This is your manual and your invoice."

"You're not going to show me how to work this thing?"

"Oh, it's real simple. Once you set it up with your personal security code, you just hit the code, press the green button to unlock, the red one to lock. It's all in the manual. We got the whole place wired, just like you asked. Every outside door and window."

She took the thick instruction booklet from the envelope, then eyed the panel on the wall.

"You have a good night now, ma'am." He nodded to the others and they gathered up their toolboxes and filed out the front door.

She watched them go, then sighing, closed the door. "It'll be morning before I get this thing figured out."

"It looks like the same system that's on my shop," Jack said. "I can probably walk you through it. If you don't mind me knowing your security code."

"Hell, if I can't trust my worst enemy, who can I trust?"

He shrugged, looking around the house, absently rubbing his arms. "So, what makes you think there's something otherworldly going on here?"

"Besides the human-blood message on my mirror, you mean?" She walked through to the kitchen and he followed. "You want coffee?"

"Love some."

"Sit."

He took a seat at the square table. It was topped in white ceramic tiles with green ivy leaves on them. She put a clean filter into the coffeemaker's basket, then opened a canister and scooped out some coffee. And she talked.

"I was soaking in the tub last night when it happened," she said softly. "The shower curtain was closed. To keep the steam in there with me." She patted her cheeks. "Good for the skin, you know."

"Right."

She slid the basket into the maker, then carried the carafe to the sink and ran water. "So, I'm soaking in the tub and all of the sudden the temperature in the bathroom just plummets. Just like that. I had goose bumps. I could see my breath."

Okay, she could see her breath. He couldn't chalk it up to her imagination, then, could he? Not if she could see her breath.

"I got out of the tub, wondering what the hell was going on. The furnace wasn't running. It should have been if it had suddenly become that cold outside. But nothing. I...I felt something. I don't know how to describe it, it's just..." She gave her head a shake. "So I went to the bedroom for my robe, but it wasn't cold in there. Just in the bathroom. And when I went back in there, those words were on the mirror."

He frowned. "So, whoever left you that message did it while you were in the next room."

She nodded. "But I never heard anything. Not a footstep, not a breath. Not the door opening—and those the hinges squeak. I should have heard something. Unless they were in the bathroom with me the whole time."

He nodded slowly. "I'm not...feeling anything now."

"No. No, neither am I." She rolled her eyes. "It's probably ridiculous. I mean, it's almost certainly some human asshole who left me that message. It's just... well, when I read the accounts from other people who've lived here over the past thirty years... I figured it wouldn't hurt to make sure."

"Accounts? You mean in that book you had?" She nodded. "What's in them?" he asked.

"Noises, lights going on and off by themselves, doors opening, furniture being moved. Burners turned on without warning. Music, footsteps. You name it, it's in there. The most common occurrence is the weeping."

"Weeping?" He got a chill at the word.

She nodded. "I haven't heard it. It's usually heard in the basement, and I can't quite bring myself to go down there, so that might be why. So? What do you think?"

"Like I said. I'm not sensing anything. Not at the moment, anyway."

She was quiet for a second. Then, "Maybe if you stay awhile. Maybe...if you come up to my bedroom—"

He looked up so fast he nearly wrenched his neck.

"And the bathroom. Where it happened."

Slowly, he nodded. "Sure. But let's have that coffee first, okay?"

She seemed to relax just a little, smiling, nodding. Then there was a sound from upstairs—something like shattering glass. Jack jumped to his feet and, amazingly, Kiley shot into his arms.

CHAPTER FIVE

*J*ack could have kicked himself. What the hell was he doing? His hands were buried in her hair and her nose was crushed in the fabric of his shirt, not an altogether unpleasant experience. Dammit. She went to pull back, but his arms slid lower, hands cradling her shoulders, almost as if he wanted to keep her there, pressed against him, body to body.

"You can let go now," she said. Or at least, that was what he *thought* she said. It sounded more like a series of grunts with her face mashed to his chest the way it was. And frankly, the heat of her breath penetrating the fabric and bathing his flesh was a little distracting.

He let her go and looked down at her, and he hoped he didn't look as confused as he felt. Because, *damn*, there had been a moment there...

He squelched the thought, figuratively licked his thumb and forefinger and snuffed that little sucker right out. So, what if it burned a little and he thought he heard the hiss? "You okay?" he asked, just so he could fill the silence and stop falling into her eyes.

"I'm fine. I'm right here in front of you, you can see I'm fine."

"I meant—"

"What the hell was that, anyway?" she asked, glancing toward the living room where the stairs were.

"I don't know."

She drew herself another step away from him. He let his hands fall from her shoulders to his sides. He hesitated only a moment before he realized she was probably waiting for him to *do* something. Then, before he could act on the realization, she said, "Well, I'll be damned if I'm too afraid to go up there and find out."

She ought to be, he thought. But then he was ashamed of himself, because she was stomping off through the house toward the staircase all alone. He followed her, caught up to her. Even put a hand on her again. He didn't plan to, it just sort of happened. His hands seemed to feel now that the ice had been broken, it was okay to touch her at will. Which, of course, it wasn't. Still, he put a hand on her shoulder, and she stopped at the bottom of the staircase and glanced over her shoulder at his face, looking mildly irritated.

"What?" she snapped.

"I'll go," he said. It came out in a deep tone that sounded rather heroic, he thought.

She rolled her eyes. "I'm going. But you can come with me if you want."

He nodded, stepped around her and started up the stairs. As if he were the big brave warrior, and she, the innocent virgin in need of his protection.

Still, he went up the stairs, down the hall. Then he stopped, uncertain which way to go.

"My bedroom is that one," she whispered, leaning closer and pointing.

"You think that's where the noise came from?" he whispered back.

She nodded, her wide eyes fixed on the bedroom door. She was scared to death and determined not to show it.

Then again, so was he. He moved toward the door, reached for the knob, put his hand on it and sucked in a breath at the iciness of the brass. Twisting all the same, he pushed the door open, stepped through—and *that* took some major willpower— and flipped on the light switch.

The first thing he saw was his breath forming little clouds in the air in front of him. He could see them. There was no mistaking it, the bedroom was that cold.

"Hell, here we go again," she whispered.

He stood very still, vaguely aware that Kiley was gripping his arm, maybe a little less concerned about hiding her fear. He felt wind hitting him in the face and glanced toward the windows, seeking an explanation for the cold, but the windows were shut tight.

Then where was that icy wind coming from?

"What the...?"

Suddenly, there was rattling, shaking. The lamp on the bedstand trembled, and the light fixture in the ceiling began to swing. The room exploded in sound and motion. Dresser drawers flew open one after the other, one of them so hard it wrenched itself out of the dresser and onto the floor, scattering its contents. The closet door flew open at the same time, as did the bathroom door, towels sailing through it as if hurled at them by unseen hands. The curtains were whipping like vipers.

Then—just as suddenly—the wind died and everything went still. The curtains fell limply, the stands and fixtures stopped trembling, the room was silent again.

Jack breathed. Maybe for the first time since turning on the light. No steam emerged from his lips now. It was over, whatever the hell it had been.

And Kiley was clutching his arm with both hands, and her body was pressed tight to his side. Given that she'd sooner cling to a spraying skunk or a rabid badger—or both—he figured she must be pretty shaken.

"I don't like you. McCain," she said. "You know that, right?"

"Right. No more than I like you, Brigham."

"And I'm *not* afraid of this thing. I'm not afraid of anything. You know that, too, right?"

He shrugged. "I've never seen you scared. I can give you that." Till now, he thought, but he didn't say that part aloud, mostly because it would piss her off and he was dying to see where the hell she was going with this.

"Good, just so we're clear on it. I wouldn't want you to take it the wrong way when I ask you to spend the night with me."

He swallowed hard, about to tell her she couldn't pay him enough to spend the night in this fucked-up house. But before he could speak, she went on.

"You're used to this, after all," she said. "You talk to the spirit world all the time, right? So you've seen this kind of shit before."

He probed her big green eyes wondering for one brief moment if she could have possibly engineered this entire event, special effects and all, just to finally trip him up. And all of a sudden, he realized he had to be very, very careful.

"Right," he said. "Not that you ever really get used to it, but yeah, I've seen it before."

The relief on her face was so intense that he thought she was close to tears.

"I don't know why the hell that should make me feel any better, especially when I still don't believe you're for real."

"But it does?" he asked.

She didn't answer that. "Will you stay? Spend the night?"

He would rather stick hot needles into his own eyes, he thought. But aloud, he said, "Sure."

She sighed, lowering her head, eyes, shoulders, all at once. "Good."

"Hey, I'll expect suitable compensation for this. Don't think I'm doing it as a favor or anything."

"No, not on your life." She met his eyes again, hers hiding just a hint of a smile. "So, do you think you can...get rid of it?"

He didn't even know what the hell *it* was. He was clueless. He'd never been within a hundred miles of a real ghost, so far as he knew. Didn't even believe in them—or hadn't, up until five minutes ago. Now he wasn't sure what to believe. "If this thing can be... banished, then I'm the guy who can do it." He was lying through his teeth.

Her shaky smile widened a little. "I'll tell you one thing, I'm not sleeping in here."

"Don't blame you there."

"Do you want to?"

"Huh?" He thought his eyeballs might have come close to popping out of his head.

She shrugged. "To get a better feel for—for whatever it is we're dealing with."

"Oh. No, there's...no need."

"Then you already know what it is?"

He nodded, deciding to say anything that came to mind, so long as it kept him from having to sleep in that room. He still had goose bumps, even though the chill had fled. "It—uh—seems like a pretty straightforward case of poltergeist activity. It's not that unusual. Not a big deal."

"Maybe not to you."

He shrugged. The genuine-looking gratitude gleaming up at him from her eyes gave him the *cojones* to move farther into the bedroom, where he bent to pick up a drawer, along with several of the items that had been flung from it. His nonchalance fled, though, when he realized he was holding a pair of panties in his hand. Something tightened in his nether regions, and he stuffed them back into the drawer and hoped she hadn't noticed.

"So, is there a guest room or something?" he asked as he

replaced the drawer in the dresser and closed all the others.
LEFT OFF

"Not furnished. We can sleep downstairs. There's a sofa bed."

He shot her a questioning look. She ignored it, swallowing something he took to be her pride when she said, "Will you wait here while I grab a nightgown?"

He nodded. "You, um...wanna shower?"

"Not in there."

He felt sorry when he saw the shudder that worked through her. "Hell, Brigham, why don't you just come back to my place with me, spend the night there? This is insane."

She met his eyes and shook her head just once. "I'm not letting this thing chase me out of my house." Then she took her gaze off him and looked around the room. "You hear that, spook? This is my damn house now. I've sunk every penny I have into it, and I couldn't leave if I wanted to. So, you and I are just gonna have to come to terms. Got it?"

Jack half expected the house to reply, even found himself looking around at the empty space, as she had been doing. But the house said nothing.

Sighing, she strode past him to the dresser, and plucked a nightie from a stack of silky fabrics without even looking down. "You have got to get rid of it for me, Jack. You do this for me, and I swear, I'll lay off you forever. Shit, I'll even do a column endorsing you as legit."

He shook his head, his gaze stuck on the nightie she held. It was emerald green, like her eyes. Satiny and smooth with spaghetti straps, and lace in the deep V of the neckline.

If he was being honest with her, he supposed he might admit that he would actually miss it if she stopped bugging him all the time, trying to get the best of him. But he wasn't being honest with her. Far from it.

And he was about to begin living the lie of a lifetime.

She hurried out of the bedroom into the hall. He followed,

pulling the bedroom door closed behind him, wishing he could lock it, wondering if locks could keep ghosts incarcerated and guessing probably not. He followed her down the hall to the stairs. On the way she opened a closet and tugged out a stack of sheets and blankets. Back downstairs, in the living room, she yanked the cushions off her sofa, and Jack assisted her in pulling it out into a bed. Then he stood there watching in some kind of surreal trance while she made up the bed. For two.

"Turn your back."

"What?"

"I want to get undressed and I'm afraid to leave the room by myself. Pathetic and stupid, I know, but there it is. So, turn around."

He turned around. "And what am I supposed to sleep in?"

"Your shorts?" she asked.

He could hear her peeling off her clothes, the fabric brushing over her skin. It was interesting, trying to guess what she was taking off, what remained. He told himself he shouldn't be having impure thoughts about his worst enemy, but then decided he was sleeping with her, so it was only natural.

She finally said, "Okay," and he turned again.

Then he saw her in the green nightie, the way it hung from her shoulders, flowing like a satin river over her skin, except for where it tripped over her breasts. He could see them clearly through the fabric, nipples and all.

"What?" she asked.

He jerked his gaze upward, to her eyes again. "You do realize you've left nearly every light in the house on?"

"And your point is?"

He shrugged. "You don't even want to brush your teeth?"

"Planning to kiss me before morning, Jack?"

"Not if you begged me, sweetie."

"Then why are you worried about it?"

"Because you might roll over and breathe on me."

She rolled her eyes. "My breath is fine. And I showered this morning. But if you need to, you can use the shower in the downstairs bathroom."

"I think I will."

"Good." She came to him, taking his hand as if he were a child being walked to the school bus for the first time. "This way." She led him through the living room, down a hallway and in through the third door on the left. "Here we go."

"Great. Thanks."

He stood there for a minute, waiting. She leaned back against the countertop, also waiting.

"Uh, were you planning to stay for this?" he asked at length.

"I can brush my teeth while you're washing up."

She didn't wait for an answer, just turned to face the sink, opened the medicine cabinet and located a toothbrush that was still in its wrapper. "I always keep extras around. There's one for you, too." She took out a second toothbrush and laid it on the counter. Then she glanced over her shoulder with a frown. "Well, go on, take your shower. I'm not going to look at you."

"You're looking at me now."

"That's because you weren't moving." She turned to face the sink again, cranked on the water.

Sighing in resignation. Jack turned on the taps, adjusted the temperature and began stripping off his clothes.

CHAPTER SIX

She kept her eyes lowered, everything in her focused on brushing her teeth as he peeled off his clothes. The mirror was dead ahead. She could catch a glimpse of him if she wanted to, but she didn't want to. Hell, she couldn't think of anything she wanted less. Besides, by the time the thought had time to pass through her mind, he was under the spray. She heard him yank the curtain shut, heard the way the flow of water changed when he stepped underneath it.

From the shower he called, "I can't believe you're too scared to even go into the bathroom by yourself."

She frowned, her eyes rising to the mirror, where she could see very little—just his shadow on the shower curtain. "I am not scared."

"No?"

"No. I just want to make sure you're close by in case anything weird happens again."

"So I can protect you?"

"So you can witness it. You're my ghost buster, after all."

"Uh-huh."

"I figure you need access to this thing so you can decipher

45

how best to deal with it. You know, which rattles to shake and which weeds to burn, that kind of shit."

"Helpful of you."

"I do what I can." She rinsed her mouth, spit, gargled, spit again. "Don't let it fool you, though. I'm no more convinced you're legit than I've ever been."

"Then why ask for my help?"

She thought on that for a long moment, then sighed. "You're the best shot I have. There's not really anyone else."

"So, it's one of those 'last man on earth' situations?"

"More like one of those 'any port in a storm' situations."

"I see."

She sighed. "So, have you?"

"Have I what?"

"Figured out which rattles to shake and which weeds to burn?"

He was quiet for a moment. "I have some ideas."

"Good. How much longer are you going to be?"

"Two minutes, why?"

She glanced at the toilet, decided not to risk it, reached for a clean washcloth and turned on the taps. "Hey!"

She looked up fast at the exclamation, realized her blasting hot water into the basin must have given him a shot of cold. "Sorry." She shut the water off. Then she smeared some of her facial cleanser on, dipped the cloth into the basin and washed her face. She was applying moisturizing night cream when she glimpsed his long, tanned arm snaking out of the shower, groping for a towel. She handed him one.

"Thanks."

"You're wel—" Before she could finish, he yanked back the curtain and stepped out of the shower. And then she was stuck there. She couldn't force her errant gaze to move from his body. Good God, it was incredible. Who would have thought such a jerk would have a body like that? Muscular shoulders, smooth and hard. Sculpted chest, and abs—oh, hell, his abs belonged in *Playgirl*. She could wash laundry on those abs.

"I'm wel...?" he asked.

"Built," she said.

"Compliments, from you?"

"More like an expression of surprise."

"Shock and awe?"

"Shock, yeah. Not so much of the awe."

He shrugged. "And what would it take to up your awe factor? Just out of curiosity, mind you."

She shrugged right back. "Hell, I don't know. Maybe if you lost the towel?"

He gaped. She grinned, and then he relaxed. "Funny," he said. He reached for his clothes, which he'd draped over the towel bar. The briefs he tugged free were small, dark blue and clingy. She finally worked up the willpower to stop gawking at him and turned around again. But she was all too aware that he was dropping the towel and pulling those briefs on, and some little devil inside was trying to talk her into peeking.

She resisted. Barely.

"You want to stay while I drain the snake?"

"Drain the...? Oh. That's the tackiest thing I've ever heard."

He shrugged and moved toward the toilet.

She darted out of the bathroom at the speed of light. But she didn't go far. After closing the door behind her, she remained right there, just outside it. Hell, it pissed her off to no end that she was afraid to be alone in her own house. But damn.

She heard the flush, the water running in the sink. Then he stepped out of the bathroom. He didn't close the door, just held it open. And stood there looking at her.

"What?"

"Oh, come on. You know you have to. Go on. I'll wait right out here."

She thinned her lips, thought about snapping at him. But he

was right. She did have to go, and as a matter of fact it was borderline decent of him to offer to stay close by while she did.

"I don't need you to wait out here for me," she said as she went into the bathroom.

"I know you don't, but I'll wait here, anyway."

If she didn't dislike him so much, she'd have been grateful. As it was, she could only wonder if he was storing up all these weaknesses he was discovering in her for future use in the unending battle between them.

When she came out again, she noticed him looking at her body, and decided she wasn't the only one with weaknesses. He looked often, every time he thought she might not notice. Could her nemesis be attracted to her? Damn, she would never let him hear the end of it if he admitted that one!

She led the way back to the living room, flung back the covers and crawled into bed. She really hadn't been worried about spending the night with Jack. Now, though...

"You aren't going to put on a T-shirt?" she asked.

"Wasn't wearing a T-shirt," he said. "Can't very well sleep in my button-down."

"I don't know why not. I could."

His eyes changed just a little, lowering slowly. And she got the distinct impression he was picturing her sleeping in his button-down shirt.

"This isn't going to be a problem, is it?" she asked, sliding to one side to make room for him.

He got into the bed beside her, pulled the covers over them both and lay back on the pillows with his hands folded behind his head. "What isn't?"

The attraction, she thought. The fact that her enemy suddenly turned her on like nobody's business and she got the feeling he was having the same reaction to her. But she wasn't going to be the first one to admit it. "Nothing," she said. "Never mind."

He nodded. "'Night, Brigham."

"'Night, McCain."

She closed her eyes, knowing good and damned well she would never sleep.

He did not seem to have the same problem. In fact, he was snoring softly within ten minutes. And five minutes after that, he rolled over, and before she knew what to expect, he had wrapped her up tight against him, imprisoning her there with one arm and one leg. Her face was pressed to his chest, one arm caught between his belly and hers, and her pelvis was mashed to his groin.

"Oh, great," she whispered.

"Mmm," he replied. And then one of his big hands burrowed into her hair, stroking just a little before settling down.

Something in her stomach turned a somersault. She tried to tug her arm from where it was trapped between them, but in the process her hand brushed over his abs, and she stopped what she was doing as her heart skipped a beat. Lifting her head away from his chest just a little, she peered up at his face. His eyes were closed, his breaths deep and steady. Sound asleep. So...

She let her palm rest lightly on his abdomen, and when he didn't stir or react, she moved it just a little, up and down over the rippling muscles there. God, he must work out like a man driven to have a belly like that. She'd never touched anything so perfect. So arousing. Too bad it was attached to a man she didn't like.

"Hey, Kiley?"

She froze, her hand going still.

"You awake?"

That was it, that was it. Just pretend to be asleep. Perfect. She tried to breathe the way a sleeper breathed, but gradually, so he wouldn't notice the sudden change.

"Kiley?"

She didn't respond, just kept breathing, kept still.

He drew his arm from around her, eased her from her side

onto her back so slowly she knew he was trying not to wake her. She guessed he didn't want her to realize he'd been holding her so...intimately.

But no, that wasn't it. A second later, she knew that wasn't it, because he was sitting up, just a little, and she felt his hand pushing her hair away from her face, slowly, softly. The warmth of his touch trailed over her jaw to her neck, to her shoulder, and slowly, slowly, lower, drifted over her satin-covered breast, making her want to slap him and arch closer all at the same time. But he kept going, sliding his hand to her belly, sideways to trace the curve of her waist, and back again to her abdomen.

Enough. Hell, it was enough. He was making her hot without even trying, and if he kept it up she was going to have an orgasm right in front of him.

She made a little noise in her throat and slowly rolled onto her side, facing away from him, just so he'd get the idea that, even asleep, she was rejecting him.

He went still for a moment. And then he was touching her again. His hands, both of them now, on the small of her back and sliding lower, boldly, right to her buttocks, cupping her cheeks and squeezing.

Furious and more turned on than she could believe, she jerked onto her other side, facing him, and said, "Just what the hell do you think you're doing?"

He smiled slowly. "Same thing you were doing to me a few minutes ago. Fair is fair."

"I don't have a clue what you're talking about. I wasn't doing anything but sleeping a few minutes ago."

"Liar." He took her hand, and slowly moved it to his abdomen again, held it there gently with his hand over it. She could've pulled away, but didn't. "Go on, touch to your heart's content. I don't mind."

"You damn well should mind. You don't even like me."

He shrugged. "I'm a guy. Liking you doesn't have to enter into it. Go on, satisfy your curiosity. Feel me up."

She slid her hand over those rock-hard abs even as she pulled it away. "You are so full of yourself."

"I'd far prefer you to be full of me."

She blinked hard and fast. "What?"

He shrugged. "We're both adults. Unmarried, uncommitted."

"One of us ought to be committed, though."

He smiled slowly, pushing her hair away from her face. "If we're not gonna be enemies anymore—are, in fact, becoming allies in the war against your spooks—then there's really no reason we shouldn't."

"There are a million reasons we shouldn't."

"You want to. I want to. It's surprising, I admit that, but—"

"I do *not* want to."

"No?" He ran the back of his hand over her breast again. "Gee, Kiley, your body says otherwise."

She narrowed her eyes on him. "I hate you."

"You want me, though. I want you, too."

"You son of a—"

His hand slid down over her belly, and she felt herself wanting it to keep going, wanting him to touch her. "Tell me to stop," he whispered.

She didn't. And he was right, liking didn't even enter into it.

His fingers touched the top of her panties. He slid them inside. "You can tell me to stop anytime, you know," he whispered again. He was leaning over her, his face very, very close to hers. "But I hope you don't."

She told herself to tell him to stop, and then tell him to go away. But instead, she felt her thighs ease a little farther apart, her hips push against his hand, just a little.

He moved his hand farther, rubbing against the softness. "Damn, woman. I haven't been this hot for anyone in ten years. Why the hell did it have to be you?"

She tried to answer, but all that came out was a soft moan, and that just made him rub her harder, exploring new places, probing to new depths. She reached for him, desperate to know this was hitting him as hard as it was hitting her, and found that it was. So she rubbed, teased him the way he was teasing her.

He drew his hand away, got up onto his hands and knees, above her. She felt cold and eager to be in his arms again. But he was kneeling over her, stripping away her panties, peeling off her nightgown, staring down at her naked body. "Hell, Brigham. You never told me you were a goddamn goddess." He closed his hands on her breasts.

She wanted him as naked and vulnerable as she was, so she tugged at his briefs until they came down and she had complete access.

He slid off the foot of the bed, grabbed her ankles and pulled her lower on the mattress until her butt was at the very edge. Then he pushed himself slowly inside her.

And then, for some reason, he went still and swore softly under his breath.

CHAPTER SEVEN

$\mathcal{T}$he lights were out. He was kneeling between her warm, firm thighs, buried inside her, every nerve ending in his body electrified. And every single light in the place had just gone out, making Jack wonder if someone had come in. Or maybe the storm going on inside him was actually happening outside, and the power had gone out.

He stopped moving, and she made a soft sound of protest. Then he wondered what the hell demon lived in this house, that it would possess him to do something as stupid as to sleep with his worst enemy. And yet, when he looked at her, lying beneath him, squirming against him, head moving side to side, eyes closed, he wanted to ignore the sudden blackout and keep up what he was doing. It would be a mistake, but damn, what a pleasant mistake to make.

He hovered there, inside her, debating, mind against body. He moved himself just a little deeper, loving the sounds she made. And then the light in the stairway flashed on, flickered, went off again. "Hell," he muttered.

"What?"

Her eyes blinked open, just as the TV set flashed on, its

volume full throttle, blasting a hard rock video. The surprise of that blast of noise sent her eyes flying wider. He withdrew from her fast, as startled as she was.

She blinked at the TV screen, then at the flickering stairway light. "Jack?"

"I'll shut it off." He went to turn off the television. The volume was deafening.

"Wait." She said it loud, then reached out and grabbed the remote from the end table beside the sofa bed. She hit the power button on the TV, and it went dark, silent. The stair light flicked again, then stayed on. One by one the other lights came back on as well.

She pursed her lips, drawing the sheet up to her chest as if suddenly embarrassed to be naked in front of him. "Maybe my ghost is the jealous type."

He smiled, not because she was funny, but because she was making jokes when she must be frightened half out of her mind. Kiley was tough, but then again, he'd always known that. "Maybe it's just as well," he said, and couldn't believe he was saying it.

"I was thinking the same thing. Sex probably isn't the best idea we ever had. We don't even like each other."

"Oh, I don't know. You're growing on me, Brigham."

"Yeah, and us being naked in the same bed has nothing to do with that whatsoever?"

"I didn't say that."

She shook her head. "Whatever just happened here—"

"Almost happened," he corrected her.

"Almost?" She pursed her lips. "We didn't finish, Jack, but we definitely got started."

"It was a goddamn good start, too."

She averted her eyes. "It wasn't based on affection. Or caring. Or any tender feelings whatsoever."

"Oh, come on. Don't pretend you can speak for me on that."

"We didn't even kiss first."

He mulled that over, realized she was right. So, no kissing, to a female, equaled no caring, no tenderness. Good to know. "Okay, so there was no kissing. If this thing that almost happened —that started to happen—wasn't based on affection, then what was it based on?"

She shrugged. "Libido? Fear? Chemistry?"

"And those are the wrong reasons to have sex?" he asked.

"All the wrong reasons. But it's okay. The ghost caught us in time."

"Gives me even more motivation to help you get rid of it," he said, sending her an evil grin.

She smiled back, and a lump formed in his throat as he watched the movement of her lips, and he realized he wanted to kiss her. He regretted not taking his time, before. Just as well, though. Hell, what would she have read into it then? Still, the thought persisted.

"Think you can sleep?" she asked. She was getting out of the bed, tugging the covers with her. He glimpsed as much of her as possible, figuring it would be his last chance for a while.

He surprised himself by answering honestly. "Not next to you, no."

She picked up her nightie, pulled it on over her head, letting the covers go only when she was concealed. Didn't matter. He'd seen her and the image was burned into his mind. He almost groaned aloud when she stepped into the panties and pulled them up.

Then she tossed him his briefs, because he was sitting there on the bed with a pillow over his privates. "Good," she said.

"Good what? That I'm not going to be able to sleep?"

"Exactly. I won't sleep, either. Between *almost* jumping your bones and the damn ghost, I'll be lucky if I can sleep again for a week."

"You sound like you have a plan—something we can do instead."

She nodded, padding across the room and taking the book she'd had in her car earlier from the fireplace mantel. He used the opportunity to pull on his underwear and prop the pillow behind his head. She said, "We can read. I already got started, but nothing that really explains any of this, so far."

She handed him the book. He looked at it and nodded. "There's an entire section on this house." She climbed back into the bed beside him. "I think I might have a case against the real estate agency. Do you?"

"Failure to disclose ghosts. Yeah, it's probably in the law books, right in the same section where they have to disclose termites and leaky roofs."

She smiled again. "Go on, open to the section. We might as well read it together, though I'm not altogether sure I want to know any more than I already do."

He nodded, flipped to the chapter that opened with a photo of her house and started reading.

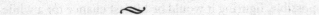

BY THE TIME they finished the section, it was nearly dawn. The "ghost" or whatever was raising hell in Kiley's new home had been quiet for the rest of the night, and she was starved.

She closed the cover. "Well, *that* was helpful."

"Not."

She stretched and got to her feet. "Hungry?"

"Don't tell me you're offering to cook me breakfast?"

"What are you, insane? You're taking me to IHOP."

He glanced at his watch. "They won't be open for an hour and a half."

She pouted. "Oh, hell. Well, I can scramble an egg, but the whites might be runny. I never seem to get them quite—"

"How about if I make breakfast?"

She raised her eyebrows.

"Yeah, I can cook. Just don't let it get around." He got up, pulled on his jeans.

She led the way to the kitchen, showed him where things were, put on a pot of coffee, then sat at the table and watched him work. He knew his way around a kitchen, whisking eggs in a large bowl, adding milk, cinnamon, nutmeg, soaking slices of bread in the concoction, and dropping them onto a sizzling griddle. "Wow," she said.

"I'm a man of many talents." He glanced at her. "As you would have found out last night, had we not been so rudely interrupted."

She let herself grin back. This was something new, this flirting going on between them. She wasn't sure how to react to it. Was this going to be the new nature of their relationship, now that she'd vowed to stop trying to discredit him and put him out of business? How odd it would seem not to be his worst nightmare anymore. She wasn't sure how to deal with it, or whether she even liked it. She'd enjoyed tormenting him.

She decided to change the subject. "Let's nutshell this, shall we?"

"Sure." He expertly flipped the French toast.

"What do we know about this house that we didn't know before?" she asked.

"Well, the last couple who lived here moved out within six months, but refused to cite a reason or be interviewed by the book's author," Jack said.

"The couple before that claimed that the place was haunted. Talked about lights and things going on and off, items being moved around, footsteps in the middle of the night."

"Nothing as drastic as what's been happening to you, though."

She nodded. "Same as the family who lived here before them. They actually liked the ghost, said it watched out for them. I wonder why. I mean, the ghost has never seemed hostile to anyone else—"

"That we know of," he said.

She nodded. "But prior to that, there was nothing—not until the suicide."

"Yeah. You know, I had no idea Phil Miller had ever lived in this house, much less that his first wife had committed suicide."

"You mean you know him?"

He nodded. "He's a music teacher in a neighboring school district. Must be close to retirement age by now. But I've seen him around."

"He comes into your shop? Seems interested in the spiritual?"

"Nah. We eat in the same diner a lot."

"Oh." She was disappointed. For a moment there, she thought she might be onto something. Then she brightened again. "Still, it was right after her death that the hauntings began. Do you think it's Sharon Miller, Jack? Do you think she's the ghost?"

He shrugged. "Need a plate, here."

She hopped up, got two plates from the cupboard and handed him one. He stacked three slices of the toast onto it, handed it back to her and threw three more onto the griddle. "Go ahead and start without me."

She set her plate on the table, went to the fridge for margarine and maple syrup, and got out a bottle of orange juice while she was at it. Then she got silverware and glasses for them, and when that was done, she poured two mugs full of coffee and set the creamer and sugar on the table.

"There."

By then he was flipping his three slices onto his plate and joining her. He sat down. She said, "So, where should we begin?"

"Well, you can tell me what your life was like before you came to Burnt Hills," he said.

She looked up quickly. "I meant with the ghost. Can you just exorcise this thing, or do you need to know more about it, first?"

He seemed to be taking his time, thinking it over while adding syrup to his toast, cream to his coffee. "Well," he said at length.

"The more information we have, the more effective the exorcism will be."

"That's what I figured. So, what's the plan?"

"Right now, eating breakfast. And talking. Where are you from, Kiley?"

She sighed. "You really wanna know?"

"Yeah. I know, it seems odd to me, too."

She shrugged, took a bite and moaned in ecstasy. When she'd swallowed, she said, "This is incredible."

"I know."

She sipped her coffee. "I was a spoiled little rich girl from Richmond, Virginia. Inherited my parents' entire fortune. Fell for a con man who married me, took me for every red cent, and then left me high and dry."

She felt his eyes on her, realized he'd stopped eating. Slowly she looked up at him.

"That's why you're so down on people you perceive to be hucksters?"

She nodded. "It's why I stopped believing anything I couldn't find proof of." She shrugged. "Maybe I've been wrong. Maybe my own bitterness has warped my vision."

"Maybe." He wasn't quite meeting her eyes anymore, and he dug back into his breakfast as if it were the most important thing he would do all day.

When she'd finished every bite and was sipping her coffee, she leaned back in her chair. "God, I feel like patting my belly. That was delicious."

"Glad I managed to satisfy at least one of your physical cravings."

She smirked at him. "Oh, I don't think you'd have had any trouble with the other."

"No?"

She didn't answer. Since when did she stroke this man's ego? Not that that's what she was doing. God, it would have been mind-blowing. But it didn't pay to think about that. It hadn't happened. It wasn't going to.

"Okay, so here's what I'm thinking," she said.

"About what?"

"About the ghost. I think we should contact the last couple who lived here."

"The ones who wouldn't talk to the author?"

She nodded. "They might be more willing to talk to me. I mean, I'm living here, after all."

"You're also a journalist who enjoys exposing people as frauds. They might be suspicious of you."

"Hmm, you have a point. Okay, so you'll have to help me talk to them. Meanwhile, we'll do a little investigative digging into Mr. Miller. See if we can find out anything more about his wife's death."

"Like what?"

"Like how she killed herself, and why. And what she might want from me. Maybe you could consult the Ouija board or whatever the hell you use, see if you can get any answers from her directly."

"Naturally. That was going to be my first move."

She nodded, swallowed more coffee. Outside the sun was coming up, its orange-yellow rays beaming in through the kitchen windows. "I suppose I should take a shower."

He nodded. "Yeah. I should wash up and shave, myself. You want me to stand in the bathroom while you shower?"

She thought that would be a bad idea. Very bad. She would be all too tempted to reach out and yank him into the water with her. "I think I'll be okay now that it's light outside. So long as I use the downstairs bathroom."

He lifted his chin, cleared his throat. "Tell you what. I'll go use the upstairs one. Just to see what happens."

"You're a better man than I am," she told him. He was either very brave or very foolish, she wasn't sure which. "Let's both leave the doors open, okay?"

"Deal."

Gathering her nerve, she cleared the table and tossed the dishes into the dishwasher, just as a delaying tactic. Then she went to her bathroom, listening to Jack's footsteps on the stairs as he went to his.

It wasn't freezing cold. That was a good sign. The sun was beaming in through the window, higher than before. The lights were working. She opened the cabinet, taking out her body wash, bath oil, shampoo, conditioner, loofah. Then, with all those items loaded in her arms, she turned to face the tub.

And then she dropped everything on the floor and screamed at the top of her lungs.

The tub was full to the brim, water sloshing over the top onto the floor. And lying there, beneath the clear, warm water, was a woman. Her blond hair floated like a nest of yellow snakes around her head. Her mouth was slightly agape. And her eyes were wide open, focused on Kiley's, and pleading.

CHAPTER EIGHT

*T*he sound of her scream split his mind wide open and let a slew of nightmarish images flow in, each more horrific than the one before. Even though he was running before the sound died, he couldn't seem to get to her fast enough.

And then he did.

She was backed into the farthest corner of the downstairs bathroom, with one hand fisted near her mouth and the other one pointing, trembling, at the tub.

He looked at the bathtub, half afraid to. But there was nothing there.

"Kiley?" He moved closer to her. "What, what is it?" When he stood right in front of her, blocking her view of the tub, her glazed eyes focused on him. "It was there. Jack, it was there, in the tub, she was—"

"Wait, wait, hold up a sec." The tempo, pitch and decibel levels of her voice had been rising steadily, and he sensed she was close to panic, so he closed his hands on her shoulders, intending to lead her out of the bathroom, into something more nearly resembling safe ground. As soon as he touched her, she fell against him, sliding her arms around his back, burying her face in his chest and holding on so tight he thought she might crack his ribs.

He buried a hand in her hair, snapped the other around her waist and tried to keep holding her that way while maneuvering them both out of the bathroom. He took her all the way through the house, and outside, to her car—she in her nightgown, and he in his jeans. He paused only long enough to snag her key ring from the hook by the door.

"What are we...?"

"Screw this. You need to get the hell out of that house. For now, just for now."

"I haven't even showered."

"You can shower at my place."

"But my clothes—"

"I'll come back and get you some."

"Alone?"

"Not on your life." He put her in her car, shut the door, went around to the driver's side and got behind the wheel. Only when they were heading down the road did he turn to face her, to ask her, "What did you see in the bathtub, Kiley?"

She sat a little straighter in the seat. "I think I know how Mrs. Miller killed herself," she said softly.

He lifted his brows. "How?"

"Drowning. In the bathtub, I think."

"And you think this because?" He was almost afraid to ask.

"Because I saw her. The tub was full of water. Overflowing, even, and she was there, lying there on the bottom. Her eyes were open and she was looking right at me." The last few words came out in a whisper.

He ached for her, literally felt pangs in his belly for her pain.

She sent him a searching look. "She was there. She was really there."

"I believe you."

"She was young, beautiful, when she died. Long honey-blond hair. Green eyes. She could've been a model."

"We're here," he said, pulling her car into his driveway. He lived in a modest-size log home, one story with a loft. Just big enough for him. He liked it, maybe more than ever before. No history, no ghosts. Not that he believed in the damn things, anyway. He stopped the car. The look of relief on Kiley's face was something to see.

He led her inside, unlocking the place, holding the door. "I'd show you around, but it would be a short trip. Kitchen's in there. Bedroom's up in the loft. Bathroom's through there, and there's a den in back. And this is the living room."

"Nice. It's nice."

"Go on, go take your shower. And then sack out in my bed for a while. You're dead on your feet."

"I should go in to work."

"Call 'em."

"Okay. Yeah. Okay, I can rest here." She looked around, sighed. "It feels good here."

"And not a ghost in sight," he said.

She smiled. "Thanks for this."

He nodded. "I need to go to the shop, see Chris, and then I'll head back to your place and pick you up a few things. Okay?"

"Don't go there alone, though."

"I won't. But I will bring you back some clothes and stuff. I'll be a couple of hours. No more. And if you need me, my cell phone number is programmed into the landline phone. Number nine."

She nodded. "I really do owe you for all of this."

He sent her an evil smile. "I fully intend to collect, Brigham, so don't fret about it too much."

❦

CHRIS WAS ALREADY TURNING the Closed sign around to the Open side when Jack walked up to the door of the shop. The kid stepped aside to let him in, but before Jack could so much as say "good morning" the questions were pouring out.

"So? What happened last night? Did you spend the night with her? Did anything happen? I thought you hated each other. What's going on, Jack?"

Jack held up two hands and hurried through the shop toward the section in the back that was devoted entirely to books. Then he stood there, perusing the rack.

"Jack?" Chris asked. "C'mon, aren't you going to tell me anything?"

Sighing, Jack looked down at the kid. "It's not good. I'll tell you that."

"No? Not even—?"

"No, not even. And don't ask again. That's none of your business. Besides, it has nothing to do with whatever the hell is haunting Kiley Brigham's house."

Chris frowned. "I, uh—thought you didn't believe in ghosts."

"Didn't. Not until last night."

Chris widened his eyes. "You saw it?"

He shook his head. "Lights flashing, drawers flying around the bedroom, doors slamming."

"So, you were in her bedroom."

He sent the kid a glare. "Part of the job."

"Job?" Then Chris went pale. "You don't mean—"

"The lady has hired me to get rid of her ghost."

"B-but...you—"

"Believe me, I know. So now I'm in a hell of a predicament. I either admit to her that I'm a fake, or I fake my way through this, fail, and then she'll know I'm a fake, anyway." He lowered his head. "And she's been burned by a fraud like me before. Hell, when she finds out the truth—" He made himself stop there, before he gave away more than he wanted to. Not that he had a clue what he'd be giving away. He was confused as hell.

Chris shrugged. "Only one way to solve this whole mess," he said. "You're just gonna have to get rid of her ghost for her."

"Oh, come on, Chris."

"It's not like you haven't done it before. You've cleared a dozen houses right in Burnt Hills alone."

"That wasn't real and you know it. I read a few books, went through the motions and eased the minds of some extremely nervous people with vivid imaginations."

"You helped them. None of them had any visitations after you finished."

"None of them had any visitations before I started."

"How can you be so sure of that?"

Jack didn't reply.

"And what about all the readings. Jack? The advice you give these people, the way it helps them?"

"It's not hard to give people good advice."

"As good as yours, and all the time? Jack, did you ever stop to think that maybe the reason Kiley Brigham can't prove you're a fraud is because you aren't?"

He rolled his eyes.

"You knew that client was a fake the other day. You knew Ms. Brigham was in the shop. Hell, I'll bet you knew there was something in her house the second you walked through the door."

"Listen, none of this matters anyway. We've got work to do. I need to find the last people who lived in that house and see if they're willing to talk to us, and I need to figure out how the hell to get rid of a ghost. A real ghost."

"The first part's easy. Brad and Cindy Stark moved to Saratoga Springs."

"You know how to reach them?"

Chris shrugged, pulled out his phone, tapped on its screen, and said, "Here you go," and turned the phone around.

Jack saw the listing, couldn't believe it was that easy as he tapped the number.

～

KILEY HAD SHOWERED, dressed in one of Jack's clean T-shirts, and then crawled into his bed and slept like a log. She only woke when something touched her cheek, gentle as a breeze, making her eyes flutter open. Jack was crouching beside the bed, looking at her oddly.

"Oh. Hi again," she said.

"I hated to wake you, but we have a date."

She blinked sleepily. "A date?"

"Yeah. Here, I brought you some clothes." He nodded toward the stack of neatly folded garments he'd placed on the nightstand.

She sat up in the bed, raking her hair with one hand. "You went back to the house?"

"Yep."

"Alone?"

He smiled sheepishly. "Hell, no. Took Chris along."

She laughed, shaking her head.

"What? That's funny?"

"Just that a guy built like you are would drag scrawny little Chris along for protection."

"I didn't take him for protection—I took him as a witness, in case something too odd to believe happened to go down, and—" He stopped there, tilted his head a little. "A body like mine, huh?"

She pressed her lips, threw back the covers and got out of the bed, though she had to slide past him to do it. He was still sitting on the edge. "So, did anything happen?"

"What? Uh, no. Nothing. Just grabbed you some clothes—although, I kind of wish I hadn't."

Frowning, she swung her gaze his way. But his eyes weren't on hers; they were sliding up and down her body instead.

He said, "You look so damn good in my T-shirt it's a shame you have to change."

"Oh, yeah? And what is it you're hoping to accomplish with that line of bull?"

He shook his head slowly. "It's not a line, Kiley. I'd have said something sooner—I just...never thought of you that way. Until last night, at least." He gave a little shrug, met her eyes with a teasing light appearing in his own. "Guess it took sleeping with you to open my eyes."

"Yeah, that'll do it every time." She held her clothes to her chest and headed into the bathroom, muttering, "Men." Then she closed the door behind her. She tried to put his words out of her mind as she dressed. It was only his libido talking. He didn't like her, much less give a damn about her. This was all based on the heat that had flared up between them in her sofa bed, and *that* had been based on nothing more than pure idiocy, combined with bowstring-taut tension and bone-chilling fear. All that adrenaline pumping. All that unbelievable shit happening in her house. Sure, they'd reacted. Why the hell wouldn't they?

It was a mistake, and it meant nothing. And God, she wanted to do it again—and not be interrupted this time.

The look in his eyes had been so intense just then. She'd felt an answering heat rise up under her skin everywhere his gaze had lingered. His voice had gone all soft and throaty, and it felt like a touch when he said her name.

"Knock it off, Brigham." She said it to her reflection, and she said it firmly.

Her reflection looked back at her, wearing the tight, low-slung jeans he'd picked out, with a small T-shirt that hugged every curve. She wondered if he'd done it on purpose.

"Did you say something?" he asked from beyond the door.

"Uh—what's this date you mentioned?" It was the only thing she could think of on short notice. Besides wondering how he would react when he saw her in the jeans, and then scolding herself for wondering. Still, her tummy tightened in anticipation.

"I found the people who lived in the house before you. Turns out Chris knew who they were. They moved out to Saratoga Springs."

She opened the bathroom door, a hairbrush in her hand. "You called them?"

He nodded.

"And they agreed to meet us?"

"For lunch today at— Holy shit. I take it back."

"You take what back?" But she already knew. She knew by the way his eyes were wandering down her body, even before he reached out to clasp her arm and draw her farther into the room, so he could walk around behind her.

"I take back wishing I hadn't brought you any clothes. How come I've never seen you in those jeans before?"

She shrugged. "You wouldn't have noticed if you had."

"A dead man would have noticed you in those."

She sighed, turned to face him and looked him square in the eye. "What the hell are you doing?"

He looked surprised, but not confused. He knew exactly what she meant and he didn't pretend otherwise. Sighing, he lowered his eyes. "Damned if I know."

"Well, do you think you could knock it off?"

"You really want me to?"

She gnawed her lip for a moment. "I don't know. But I do know it keeps me so off balance I can't think straight. It's damn surreal to have my worst enemy flirting with me. Almost as fucked up as the ghost in my house."

"Yeah. Okay, I get that. Although I think we're way past that "worst enemy" stage. It's bull and we both know it."

She lowered her head. "Okay, it's bull."

"I never hated you as much as I pretended to."

"Me, neither," she admitted.

"It feels odd to me, Kiley, to be so into you all of a sudden. But I am."

She looked at him, questioning him with her eyes.

"I'm still not sure if you really want me to rein it in."

Kiley sighed, looking away. "Hell, neither am I."

He lifted his brows, tipped his head to one side. "Maybe if we just did it, got it out of our systems..."

She looked at the clock on the nightstand. "That's such a freakin' brilliant idea, it's a crying shame we don't have time."

"You're being sarcastic."

"No, I mean it. I'd bang you right here if it wasn't already twenty to twelve. 'Cause God knows that would fix everything."

"I never said it would fix everything."

"Asshole."

"Witch."

She held his gaze, then smiled slowly. "Now, *that* feels normal." Then she preceded him out of the bedroom and down to the car.

CHAPTER NINE

*J*ack sat across from the couple he couldn't stop thinking of as Ken and Barbie, and watched their eyes as they spoke.

"I really don't know why we agreed to this. It's kind of silly," Cindy Stark said.

"You agreed because I told you there's a perfectly nice, innocent woman living in that house now, and that she's going through hell," Jack said. "You agreed because I laid a big guilt trip on you."

The woman met her husband's eyes. "Still, that's got nothing to do with us." She slanted her gaze toward Kiley. "Whatever you're going through, it's got nothing to do with us."

"I know that," Kiley said. "But if you could just tell me what happened to drive you out of that house...?"

"Nothing drove us out," her husband Brad said with a nervous laugh. "We found a great place in the Springs."

"Oh, it's gorgeous," Cindy beamed. "Totally restored Victorian. We did it in white, with mint, rose, and lavender trim."

Jack nodded, translating their words. "You have a nice, clean, spook-free life now, and you don't want to pollute it with thoughts about the trouble you left behind. It's almost as if you might accidentally conjure the same nightmare in the new place if you admit to what happened in the old one."

Cindy widened her eyes. "How can you—how does he...?"

"Don't be silly, dear," Brad said, silencing her by covering her hand with his own. "He's taking shots in the dark."

"No," she whispered. "He's reading my mind." Kiley shot Jack a look, surprise or something like it in her eyes. Then she moved her gaze back to Cindy's. "He's going to help me clear the house."

"It's not going to work. We had three different people come in and try to clear it, but nothing worked."

"They were probably frauds. But if this can be done, Jack's the guy who can do it," Kiley went on. "The thing is, our chances of success are much better if we can figure out what's really going on. We need to know what happened. What did you see, what did you hear, what did you feel in that house?"

Brad looked at Cindy, willing her not to say a word.

Jack said, "Knock it off, pal. If you don't want to help us, that's your choice. Don't try to make her responsible for your bad karma."

Brad rolled his eyes and looked away. "I don't believe in karma."

"I do," Cindy said. "I believe in a lot of things I never did before." She looked right at Kiley. "There's more than one ghost in that house, Ms. Brigham. There's the woman in the tub, she's the main one."

"You saw her, too?" Kiley whispered.

Cindy nodded. "Once in the upstairs bath, once in the downstairs. But there are others. So many others. And some of them are angry. Some of them—lash out."

"Where have you seen these others?"

"We never saw them," Brad said softly. Almost as if the ghost might be listening. "But there were—incidents. Mostly in the cellar, but once in a while they'd come into the main parts of the house. Threaten us. Shit like that."

"Not us," Cindy said. "Just you, Brad. They never tried to harm or frighten me the way they did you."

"What did they do to you?" Jack asked.

Brad lowered his head, shook it.

"There was the time he was going down the cellar stairs to check a circuit breaker," Cindy said. "The light bulb exploded. He was in total darkness, and when he turned to come back up for a flashlight, there was a wound-up piece of wire on the stairs."

"I'd have sworn it wasn't there when I went down," he said.

"You fell?" Kiley asked.

He nodded. "Broke a leg and two ribs."

"And the incident with the water heater," Cindy went on. It was like the dam had broken for her. "The way the pilot kept going out, the matches kept blowing out, the gas was running into the cellar. And when Brad tried to come up the stairs, the door was jammed. Wouldn't open."

"My God, how did you get out?" Kiley asked.

"I don't know. Eventually they just...let me."

"Like they didn't want you dead," Jack said. "Like they just wanted you to pay attention. What do you do for a living?"

Brad Stark looked up slowly. "I'm a cop."

KILEY SPENT the afternoon at her office, trying to at least look as if she was working on a story. But the pages she keyed into her computer were not work. Not the kind she was paid to do, at least. Instead, she was creating a detailed account of everything that had been happening in her house, everything she had learned and everything she feared.

It accomplished little, she decided later on. In fact, it accomplished nothing, except to keep her mind focused on her fears.

She supposed that was better than leaving it focused on the change in her relationship with Jack McCain, which was something that scared her more than any ghost ever could. What the hell was up with that, anyway?

Sighing, she glanced at the clock, realized the day was spent and thought it was time to go home. Then she shivered. Damn, but she didn't want to go back there. And yet, she straightened her spine and got to her feet. She was not going to let anything scare her out of her home. She was not going to become so needy that she couldn't go into her own house without a chaperone. No way in hell.

She shut down her computer, shouldered her purse and picked up her keys. Fifteen minutes later, she was standing beside her car, staring at the house. The lights were still on. She'd never turned them off. She was glad of that, even though it was still dusk. The house's backdrop was a purple sky, and trees showing more skin than they had been when she'd left. Taking a breath, she marched up to the door, punched in her access code, and went inside. And then she stood there with the door wide open and the entire house spread out before her. Empty, she told herself. But it didn't feel empty. It felt as if there were eyes on her, watching her, waiting.

Kiley looked around the empty house. "Listen up, okay?" She said the words loudly and felt like an idiot for standing in her open doorway talking to herself. "I don't even know if you can hear me, but if you can I have something to say, so pay attention."

She felt something. Or maybe it was her imagination. Whatever, her courage rose a notch, and she found herself stepping farther inside. "I know you're here. I know there's something wrong, something you want me to understand. I know that now. And I'm going to find out what it is. I'm going to do everything I can to figure it out and make it right. I'm going to dig until I uncover the truth, and—" She stopped there, because a vase tipped right off a stand and shattered on the floor.

Kiley jerked backward, almost turned and fled right back through the door, but then she stopped herself. "What?" she asked. "Something I said?"

Nothing. No sound.

"Okay, then. Okay. I just...wanted to let you know I'm on your side, here. All right?"

She listened, half expecting the ghost or whatever the hell it was to reply. But it didn't.

"Of course, if you hurt me, or scare me out of the house, the deal's off. So, how about you give it a rest for a while, give me a few days to get to the bottom of this?" Again, there was no reply. Then again, she hadn't really expected one. She sighed and moved through to the living room, sinking into a chair and sighing again. "I'll be fine here by myself," she muttered. "Until I have to use the bathroom. What the hell am I supposed to do then?"

"Kiley?"

She lifted her head, startled by the voice calling her name, but only for a brief instant. It was only Jack. He stood in the doorway, a large pizza box balanced on one hand, a brown paper bag in the other.

She shouldn't be so damned glad to see him. And yet she had to fight to keep herself from smiling ear to ear and running to him.

"I stopped by the office, but you'd already left."

"Figured I had to face it sooner or later. You didn't have to come, Jack."

"I couldn't have slept a wink with you out here alone. Besides, I've been doing some research, and I think I have an idea."

"Yeah?"

He nodded, striding through the formal dining room and into the cozier kitchen. She followed him.

"Sit," he said. "I brought dinner." He put the pizza box on the table, set down the bag, and then went to the cupboards for plates and tall glasses.

"Health food, I see."

"Hell, yeah."

She peeked inside the bag, found a six-pack of cola and a large bag of potato chips, and smiled. "What, no tofu? No herbal tea?"

He put the plates on the table, went to the fridge and filled both glasses with ice. He glanced her way, seemed a little nervous.

"What is it, Jack? What's wrong?"

He sighed. "I...don't really eat tofu and bean sprouts or drink herbal tea. You were right about that stuff. And I'm telling you this now, because it's suddenly very important to me that you not think of me as some garden variety con man. So, I figure honesty is the best policy."

"So...the flaky fake diet is just to go with the image?"

"Exactly."

She sighed, flipped open the pizza box, pulled out a gooey slice and put it onto her plate.

"You're...disappointed," he said.

"No. Actually, I'm relieved. Just...worried."

"Relieved?"

She almost told him she couldn't imagine herself being with a man who subsisted on nuts and twigs, but she bit her tongue in time. "Never mind why I'm relieved. It's why I'm worried that's important here."

"Okay, then why are you worried?"

She looked across the table at him. "I'm worried about whether the rest of your claims are just as false. Tell me the truth, Jack. Can you help me, or are you just playing along to keep me from finally getting the goods on you?"

He lowered his head. "If I can't help you, Kiley, then I don't know who can." Then he met her eyes again. "To be honest. I've never dealt with anything like what's going on here in this house before. I really don't know if I can do it. After tonight, though, maybe you and I will both know."

She looked at him warily. "What happens tonight?"

"You aren't throwing me out?"

She smiled a little, shook her head. "I appreciate you being straight with me. Now, will you tell me what you have planned for tonight?"

He seemed to relax, took a bite of his pizza, then chewed while pouring cola into both their glasses. After a long drink, he said, "Tonight, Ms. Brigham, we are going to hold a seance."

Kiley blinked and held his gaze. "A seance," she repeated. "Like, where you conjure up spirits from the other side?"

"Exactly."

She blinked twice. "Jack, we already *have* spirits from the other side. What we need to do is boot them out, not invite their friends for a sleepover."

He nodded, smiling a little, an act that made his lips far more attractive than they should have been. "When we figure out what the ghosts are trying to tell us, we'll know how to get rid of them, right?"

"I... guess."

"So, we hold a séance to give them the opportunity to tell us."

"And we're going to do this ourselves? Just the two of us?"

He averted his eyes. "Well, I tried to get some of the local mediums to help us out, but seeing as how they've all been the subjects of your columns at one point or another, they all said thanks, but no thanks."

She thinned her lips, lowered her head. "They didn't put it quite that nicely, did they?"

"No. I think one of the more memorable phrases was, I hope the ghost eats her skinny white ass."

"Well, I don't blame them, I suppose. But then again, why would I want any of them? I caught each and every one of them faking, otherwise they wouldn't have made my column in the first place."

Jack hooked a finger under her chin to urge her to look him in the eye. "Just because they weren't one hundred percent genuine, Brigham, that doesn't mean they were one hundred percent phony."

"No?"

"No. This isn't black and white. There are shades of gray. All kinds of them, apparently."

"You sound surprised by that."

"I never used to believe it. Then again, until recently, I'd never—"

He stopped himself. She could almost see him stomping on a mental brake pedal. "You'd never what?" she asked.

Jack shook his head. "Nothing. Never mind, it doesn't matter. What matters is that we make this work."

"You think it will?"

"I think neither of us has any better ideas. Do we?"

She gnawed her lower lip. "I tried to contact Mr. Miller today, but he wouldn't take my call, much less return it. He wants nothing to do with this place."

"Then we're left with the ghosts. We can't solve this unless they tell us what it's about. No one else will."

She closed her eyes, then opened them again when she felt his hand sliding over hers on the table.

"I know you're scared," he said.

"I'm not—"

"The hell you're not. I'm scared too, Kiley. And not just about the damn ghosts."

Her eyebrows arched and she stared down at their hands. Then, jittery for reasons beyond her understanding, she got up from the table, slipping her hand from beneath his, turned and began pacing across the room.

Jack got up, came behind her. Very close behind her. "I want this thing solved as much as you do," he said. "I want to get it out of the way, so I can see what's left when it's gone."

"I don't know what you mean," she said, turning to face him as she spoke.

"Yeah, you do." He lifted a hand and gently pushed her hair away from her face, tucking it behind her ear.

Then, slowly, he lowered his head, brushed her lips with his. Once, then again.

Kiley's heart fluttered and her stomach tied itself in knots. The soft, tender kisses went on, until, trembling, she slid her hands up his chest, over his shoulders, and then linked her arms around his neck. His arms closed around her waist, and he pulled her tight to him and kissed her long and deeply. She let her lips part, tasting him, loving it.

Finally, he lifted his head away, and when she opened her eyes she found his probing them. Kiley tasted him on her lips and sought words and heard herself muttering, "B-but I don't even like you."

He smiled, and it made her want to kiss him all over again. "Yeah, you keep telling yourself that, Brigham. But trust me, it isn't gonna change a thing. Didn't for me, anyway." He leaned in, nibbling at her mouth again. "And you can get rid of that notion that there's no affection involved here. We kissed this time."

"Is that why you kissed me? To prove it's not just physical so you can get me into bed?"

"No. I kissed you because I wanted to. I'd like to keep on kissing you all night. But we've got other things to worry about, unfortunately."

Kiley wanted him. She wanted to make love to him right then. She pushed her hands through her hair. "This is so much to deal with. And with everything else going on—ghosts and hauntings and dead women in my bathtub—"

He nodded, taking his arms from around her waist. "I know. I'm sorry, Kiley, I shouldn't have—no. Hell, no. I'm not sorry."

She smiled up at him. "I'm not, either."

"Good. So now maybe you understand why I'm in such a hurry to get all the other stuff out of the way."

She nodded. "Yeah. Okay. So...we'll have the seance."

"Great. I've got everything we need out in the car." He turned as if to go out and fetch his props.

"No, Jack," she said, stopping him in his tracks.

He turned to face her. "Don't tell me you've changed your mind."

She shook her head. "We're not doing anything until I've finished my pizza."

CHAPTER TEN

$\mathcal{J}$ack was setting up the table in the formal dining room, feeling more nervous than he'd ever been in his life, when the doorbell chimed. Kiley was in the kitchen, putting away the leftover pizza and stacking the dishes in the dishwasher. So, he went to the door and pulled it open.

Chris stood there smiling. Behind him were two of the psychics Kiley had nailed in her column over the past year. Maya, a thirtysomething witch, blond, blue-eyed and petite, nodded hello to him as he stepped aside to let them in. She wore jeans, a cozy-looking sweater, and a pentacle around her neck. Right behind her was John Redhawk, a shaman. Aside from the turquoise beads and ponytail, he, too, was dressed casually, jeans and a green polo shirt under a denim jacket.

Jack heard Kiley come in from the kitchen. She started to say something, then stopped in her tracks.

To break the awkward silence. Jack said, "I, uh— thought you two couldn't make it."

John Redhawk sent a tight look at Kiley. "If there are spirits trapped here, they need help to get across."

Maya nodded. "We can't punish them for her actions."

"Great," Kiley said. "They're on the goddamn ghosts' side."

"Fortunately, your interests and the ghosts' are the same," John said, moving farther into the room. "As are your goals and ours—to free them, so they can move on."

Jack turned to Kiley, knowing she was about to roll her eyes or make some sarcastic comment. But he caught her in time.

"No doubt, Ms. Brigham, you think we can't be of any help anyway," Maya said.

Kiley pursed her lips. "I did catch you faking."

"You caught us being inaccurate," John explained. "There's a very big difference."

"You totally ignored all the times we were dead on target with our work," Maya added, "and focused only on the times when we missed the mark."

Chris nodded hard, then put his own two cents in. "You didn't to take into account all the people they helped. And no one was ever harmed by what they did."

Kiley lowered her head. "I get it, Chris." Then she lifted her eyes again, took a breath. "You two just admitted you're not always right. I suppose I need to do the same."

John nodded slowly. "Some of the people you condemned in your column were outright frauds, Ms. Brigham. Some of them were doing harm, and were sorely in need of exposure. I was glad to see them go. They make the rest of us look bad. But it's a mistake to paint all light workers with the same brush. And it's just as bad to hold us up to standards that are impossible for any human to meet."

She nodded. "I'm starting to realize that." Then she frowned. "But if you're not batting a thousand, then how the hell can an outsider ever tell the difference?"

"They can't," Maya said. "But we can. We know who's for real and who's just running a scam to make a buck. Maybe in the future, you could work with us, instead of against us."

Kiley blinked, clearly stunned. "You...would do that? Work with me? My God, I never thought you'd work with me."

"Because you never asked," John said. "But believe me, we'd love to help you put the frauds out of business."

Kiley shook her head in something that looked like wonder.

"Chris filled us in on the details," Maya said, changing the subject. "So, where are we doing this?"

"I'm setting up in the dining room." Jack led the way, looking with hypercritical eyes at the stuff he'd set up. Candles around the room in holders, lots of them, all white. Charcoal tablets, already lit and turning slowly white with heat, filled censers in various spots, each with a small dish of herbs beside it.

"Anything else you want to have in here?" he asked.

John lifted a dish of the herbs. "What are you using?"

"Dandelion, sweetgrass and thistle," Jack said. He'd consulted every book in his shop and taken a consensus.

"Mmm." John tugged a pouch from his jacket pocket. "I'll add a little tobacco. I've had good results with it."

"And vervain," Maya said, adding a pinch of something from her own knapsack. "To make it go." She looked around the room. "I'd feel better if we did this within a properly cast circle."

John nodded his agreement. "We'll need salt and something to represent the elements."

Chris looked at Kiley. "C'mon, I'll tell you what we need and you can help me find it." The two of them went into the kitchen.

Jack sighed, turning to the others. "Thanks for coming. I mean it, I'm in way over my head here."

"Why?" Maya asked. "It's not as if you haven't done this before."

Jack glanced toward the kitchen. "I always assumed the problem was in the minds of the clients. That's where I solved it. Hell, I went through the motions, but I wasn't really doing anything. You know that, you just finished saying you could tell the real psychics from the frauds."

They looked at each other, then slowly back at him. John said, "We can, Jack. And you're one of the real ones."

He stood there gaping until Kiley and Chris returned. She carried a bowl of water, and he had a box of salt.

"Good," Maya said. "Set the bowl in the west—that would be over here." She pointed. "Move one of those censers so it sits opposite it, in the east, and put one of the taper candles in the south." She took the salt from Chris, and poured a small pile of it in the north position. "Salt in the north, to represent Earth. Ready, everyone?"

Kiley looked at Jack. He found himself moving closer, taking her hand. "We're ready."

John was moving around the room, lighting each candle, and adding pinches of the herbal mixture to each censer. Chris shut off the lights. Then they took their seats around the table, as Maya walked in a large circle around them, pouring a boundary line of salt as she moved. When it was all poured, she set the salt box down and walked the perimeter again, moving her hands like a mime as she created an invisible sphere of protection and power.

When she took her seat at the table, all was silent.

John looked at Jack. "Take the lead, brother. This is your project, we're just here for backup."

Jack almost refused, but then he realized how that would look to Kiley. Even though he thought things had changed between them, he wasn't ready to admit to her that he was a fraud. He was terrified—not that she would expose him. Hell, he didn't even care about that anymore. No, his greatest fear was that she would turn away from him. And he didn't think he could stand that. So much more than his business was at stake. He cared what she thought of him.

He took a breath, tried to remember all the usual mumbo jumbo, and said, "Join hands." Beside him, Kiley slid her hand into his. Impulsively, he drew it to his lips, and pressed a kiss there. She squeezed a reply. He closed his eyes and instructed everyone through several deep breaths, until he felt himself slipping into a more relaxed state. Finally, he addressed the spirits.

"Those of us here at this table call out to those of you elsewhere in this house. We know you're here. We know you have something you want to tell us. We've created this sacred space and we invite you in. You are welcome here, provided you mean us no harm. You are welcome here, so long as your intentions are for the highest good. Come now, join us."

A door slammed.

Jack's head came up, eyes flying open and he saw the others on high alert. They met each other's eyes around the room, in the flickering candle glow. Suddenly, a gust of icy wind blew through, and every candle in the room went out.

Jack felt himself sinking, as if his chair had dissolved beneath him. He fought it, tried to cling more tightly to the hands on either side of him, but it was no use. They fell away and he plummeted downward, right through the floorboards, hitting the basement floor so hard it knocked the wind out of him.

He swore and got up, brushing himself off, rubbing his tailbone gingerly. Looking up, he expected to see the hole above him, but the ceiling was perfect, and draped in unbroken cobwebs.

And then he heard someone speaking softly and he turned to look behind him.

There in the corner was a man of perhaps thirty. His slicked-back hair and dated glasses made him look like something out of a '70s sitcom. Knife-sharp crease on his plaid pants, thick belt with an oversized buckle and a tie so wide it was almost funny.

Jack said, "Hey. Who the hell are you and what are you doing down here?"

But the man didn't hear him. He went right on with what he was doing. And what he was doing, Jack realized, was smoothing new concrete over a portion of the floor. He knelt there, moving a trowel over the smooth, slick gray mush.

Jack strode across to him. "What the hell are you doing?" he demanded. And when the man didn't answer, he reached for him to spin him around and make him talk. But his hand moved right through the guy.

"Jack?"

The voice was Kiley's. It was coming from above.

"Jack, are you all right? Come on. Jack, wake up!"

He felt her hands on his face, her breath on his skin. And then he was rising as if on a high-speed elevator, leaving his stomach somewhere below. He jerked his head up, opened his eyes. Kiley was standing over him. The lights were on. Maya, John and Chris surrounded him. "What happened?" he asked no one in particular.

"You passed out," Kiley said.

"He went into a trance," Maya corrected.

"He left his body, journeyed into the realm of the spirits," John put in.

"Well? Which is it, Jack? What happened to you?"

He sat up straighter in the chair, rubbed his forehead. "How long was I out?"

"Fifteen minutes or so," Kiley said.

"It felt like fifteen seconds."

She touched his face. "Are you okay? I knew this was a bad idea. I just knew it."

Jack shook his head fast. "No. No, it was a good idea. I saw something."

She frowned, staring at him. "What?"

"I think it was Mr. Miller. Only younger. He was spreading concrete in the cellar."

CHAPTER ELEVEN

Kiley stood over the sofa, where she'd made Jack lie down. John, Maya and Chris had left, at Jack's insistence. He swore he knew what he needed to know now, thanked them for their help and told them to go.

"I'm not sure what happened back there," she said.

He closed his eyes and pressed a hand to his forehead. "Neither am I. Only thing I am sure of, is that I need to see your basement."

An icy shiver rippled through her entire being. "I don't know if that's such a good idea."

"I think it's the only way to end this thing, Kiley."

"But it's not safe down there. Remember Cindy Stark's story."

"You stay up here. I just need to take a look."

Firming her jaw, she shook her head. "No. Not alone. If you're going down there, I'm going with you."

He studied her face for a moment. "You sure?"

She nodded.

Sighing, Jack reached out to cup her cheek. It was a touch that seemed tender. "You're braver than you look, you know that?"

"Is that supposed to pass for a compliment?"

"Just a fact." He got to his feet.

"Oh," she said. "You meant, right now?"

"No. No, not right yet. There's something else, first."

"Is there?"

He smiled softly, reached for her and pulled her to him. "This." He cupped her face and tipped it, so that he could kiss her the way it suited him. He took his time, tasted and explored. Kiley felt herself melting into him.

"Jack," she whispered.

"I know. This is no time for—but God, Kiley, I can't stop thinking about how it felt when we—"

"I know. I know, me too."

He slid his hands down to her waist, then up again, raising her T-shirt with them. She lifted her arms overhead, so he could take it off her. They fell onto the sofa together, clumsily undressing each other, kissing, and touching. But this time they didn't stop. And this time, the ghosts didn't interrupt.

EVENTUALLY, he slid onto his side, pulling her close, wrapping her in his arms. "That was incredible."

"It was supernatural," she agreed. "Why did we waste so much time hating each other?"

He leaned up, kissed her earlobe and held her for another ten minutes while their heart rates returned to normal. And then, finally, Kiley sighed and got to her feet. "Shall we get this over with?" she asked.

"It's as good a time as any." He got up, found their clothes, helped her to dress. Every touch was a caress. He repeated the process with the T-shirt. She took the jeans from him, because if he kept this up, he was going to make her decide to do something else besides explore the terrifying basement that might try to kill them.

Hell, what was this now? Were they casual sex partners, or something more?

She looked past him at the darkened windows, heard the wind picking up outside. Branches moved, scraping gnarled limbs over the sides of the house, like demons trying to claw their way in. She shivered, all the fears he'd made her forget returning in force. "By morning, the trees will be all but bare."

Jack slid an arm around her shoulders. "Don't worry, Kiley. I'm not going to let anything happen to you. Especially not now."

The way his voice thickened on those words made her look up at him quickly. "Don't wax mushy on me, Jack. That would be scarier than the basement."

"Come on."

She walked with him, wished he couldn't feel her shaking, but not so much that she would give up the reassuring arm around her. In fact, she walked as close beside him as she could. At the basement door, she drew a breath.

Jack reached out, closed his hand on the knob, and opened the door. She stared into a rectangle of utter blackness. Then she reached past him, into the inky dark, which felt like a physical thing, cold and dense. She found the light switch, flicked it.

Light flooded the stairway. She swallowed her fear. "We're coming down here to keep our promise, ghost. We're checking out the things you've been trying to tell us, but I'll tell you right now, at the first sign you're fucking with us, we're out of here. Understood?"

There was no sound, no sign of any reply.

She looked at Jack. He nodded. "Let's go, then." Still holding her near his side, he started down the stairway. It was a solid stairway, modern, obviously not the original set. They walked down, thirteen stairs, to the bottom, a smooth concrete floor.

"So?" she asked. "Where was it you saw in this... vision?"

He looked at the ceiling, evenly spaced studs, with cross-pieces in between them. Steel pipe ran along the edges of some boards, laying a hot-and-cold running trail from the basement to the bathrooms and the kitchen above. Then he lowered his gaze, scanning the basement. "Over here, I think."

She walked with him across the basement. He moved slowly, and Kiley wondered if he was feeling the same things she was. It seemed to grow colder with every step they took. And there was something else in the air. Something electric and alive.

He stopped and stared at the floor.

"Is this it?"

"Yeah. I think so."

"What do you think we should do about it?"

He sighed, looking around the room. She followed his gaze. There were some old tools hanging from hooks in the wall. Hoe, rake, shovel. They were old, battered, dusty. They'd been here when she bought the place, and she hadn't bothered to get rid of them. She hadn't even touched them. Hell, she'd only been in the basement once, with the real estate agent. For some reason she hadn't been able to venture back down there since she'd moved in.

He seemed about to answer her, when a loud clattering sound made Kiley jump six inches and clutch her chest. The old shovel lay on the concrete floor. It had fallen off its hook. She swallowed her fear, took a calming breath and looked up at Jack.

He said, "I think we need to dig up the floor."

"Yeah, I kind of picked up on that."

He nodded. "We'll need something stronger than a shovel to break through concrete." Taking her hand, he turned and started back toward the stairway.

From the corner of her eye, Kiley saw something flying toward them. She swung a hand to the back of Jack's head, pushing him forward and down, ducking along with him, and the thing whizzed over their heads so fast and so close that she felt the breeze it caused, heard the sound of it passing. It slammed into the wall on the other side of them and stayed there.

"Holy hell!" Jack straightened, staring.

She stared, too. The rounded end of the shovel was embedded in the wall, its handle sticking straight out, still quivering from the impact.

"That could have taken off your head," Kiley whispered.

"Yeah." He was staring behind him, eyes wide and watchful.

"Goddamn it!" Kiley turned and shouted. "What are you, stupid or something? We can't dig the effing floor up with a shovel. It's concrete, you idiot. We're going to need a jackhammer or something. So unless you've got one of those to hurl at us, knock it the hell off!"

Jack stared at her, then looked around the basement.

Kiley blew a piece of hair off her cheek. "You think it got the message?"

"Hell, you scared *me*. Should've worked on the ghost."

She searched his eyes, suddenly, acutely aware of how ridiculously much he had come to mean to her. "It better have," she said. She leaned up and kissed his chin.

Then, turning, they took another step toward the stairs. Nothing happened, so they started up them. They made it almost all the way to the top, before the creaking, splitting, cracking sounds alerted them to trouble. Jack grabbed her waist and shoved her ahead of him and through the stair door. Then he fell away behind her. Kiley shrieked and spun around in time to see the entire staircase collapsing, taking him with it.

"Jack!" She reached for him and the door slammed in her face.

JACK HIT THE FLOOR HARD, then curled into a protective ball as debris rained down on him. He was pummeled, his head, back, shoulders, his hands and arms where he clutched them around his face like a makeshift helmet, pounded by falling debris. He thought he heard Kiley screaming his name, but he couldn't be sure with the roar around him. And then, suddenly, there was just silence.

He tried to move. It hurt when he straightened. Boards fell off his body, clattering to the floor around him. He got upright, brushed off some of the dust and tried to take stock. His shoulder throbbed. Lower back wasn't feeling too pleasant, either. Above him, he could hear Kiley, pounding on the door, shouting and swearing.

He cupped his hands and hollered in her direction. It took two or three tries before she heard him and stopped her own shouting to listen. "Jack?" she called.

"I'm okay."

"Thank God."

He lowered his head, smiling a little at the level of relief that came through in that one simple declaration. "Jack, I can't get the door open." But he was looking at the floor by then, frowning at the way the debris had come to rest on the other side of the basement. Broken boards formed a rectangle, framing the area where he'd seen the man laying concrete. He walked over there, bending low, moving the boards away. Frowning, he looked more closely.

"Jack?"

"Just a sec!" he called.

He bent closer, noticing the way the dust had gathered into a tiny crevice, which, like the broken boards, formed a rectangle in the floor. He brushed at the dust, running his fingers along the fissure, realizing this piece of concrete was separate from the rest, not a part of the floor, but something else.

He looked across the room then, at the forgotten tools in the corner. Spotted a crowbar. "Okay, I get it," he said softly. "We don't need a jackhammer."

He heard a soft creaking sound and turned to see the cellar door swinging slowly open. On the other side, Kiley stood with a baseball bat in her hands, and it was raised up as if she'd been about to pound the door with it. She blinked down at him.

He said, "Is there another way in and out of here?"

"A hatchway door that leads outside," she said, nodding toward it. "You going to come out that way, Jack?"

"I'm afraid if I try, that exit will get annihilated, too. No, I think we need to dig this thing up now."

"But—"

"The cement's sectioned here. I think I can pry it up."

She stared at him, then at the area around him. "What, you couldn't just say so? You had to risk killing him?"

The lights flickered off, then on again. Jack said, "Maybe you should stop yelling at them, Kiley?"

"Fuck them. I'm coming back down. See you in a minute."

She vanished from the doorway. Jack went to the corner to grab the crowbar, then tugged the shovel from where it was embedded in the wall and carried both back to the spot with him.

A few minutes later, Kiley arrived at his side. She had found another crowbar and knelt on the basement floor beside him. "Are you really okay?"

"Yeah. I'll be a little sore, but nothing serious." He was jamming the flat end of the bar into the crack, moving it back and forth. The crack grew wider with every movement.

She did what he was doing, working in the other direction, and they made their way around the entire rectangle. She said, "You have a little blood on your face."

"A few of the boards landed on me when the stairs collapsed."

She kept looking at him and frowning. He smiled. "It does my ego a world of good to know you care."

"It's not by choice."

The edge he was prying rose up a little. "Here, quick, get your bar over here," he said.

Kiley hurried to his side and jammed her bar underneath, helping him pry the slab of concrete upward. Jack dropped his own bar, gripping the edge with his hands, pushing and lifting.

Kiley used her bar to help him, until finally they managed to overturn the slab. It hit the floor and split into several pieces.

Jack looked at Kiley and she handed him the shovel. He eyed the dirt that had been covered by the slab, and began scraping it aside with the shovel blade. Right away, he felt something underneath. "It's shallow," he said.

"It's cold again. Hell, Jack, I can see your breath." Kiley rubbed her arms. "We must be close."

Jack continued scraping away the soil, revealing a square of metal, two feet by two feet.

"What is it? A box, is it some kind of box?" He ran his hands over the thing, tracing its edges. "I feel...hinges." He lifted his eyes to meet hers. "Jesus, Kiley, I think it's some kind of a...door."

"A door?"

He nodded.

"A door to what?"

Damn good question. The word hell popped into his mind, but he decided not to share that with her.

CHAPTER TWELVE

"*J*ack, I'm afraid." For once Kiley didn't mind admitting it, as she stood there staring down into pitch-black darkness.

"Me, too."

"I think it's time we call the police. Don't you?"

He shrugged. "No proof a crime's been committed." He glanced down into the darkness. "Though I'd bet the farm on it."

She gripped his arm, as if she could convince him by squeezing her words into him. "Let's at least try. If the police won't come out here, then we'll do it ourselves."

He tipped his head to one side, started to speak, but then seemed to decide against it.

"Come on, Jack. We'll call the police, we'll do it right now."

He nodded, so she tugged him away from that inky maw and toward the shallow concrete steps that led up out of the cellar to an angled hatchway door. She pressed her palms to it, to push it open. But it wouldn't budge. "I know it's not locked. I thought I left it wide open, but—" She pushed again.

Jack said, "I was afraid of something like this."

She frowned at him, then she understood. "They won't let us out, will they? Not even if it's to tell their story."

"They don't trust us, Kiley. What's to stop us from getting out of here and running like hell? Never looking back? That's what everyone else who's lived here has done."

She turned slowly to face the now-open metal trapdoor in the floor. "I don't want to go down there."

"I know. Neither do I."

"Do we even have a light?"

"Yeah." He pulled a flashlight from somewhere. "I remembered about the lights going out before. Brought backup."

"Good thinking."

He took a breath. "Stay up here, Brigham. As close to the hatchway door as you can."

She shook her head. "I'm more afraid to be here alone than I am to go down there with you. We do this together."

"If you're sure..."

She gave a firm nod.

"Okay, then." He put her behind him, drawing her hands to his waist just above his hips, and she knew it was because there wasn't enough room for them to go side by side down the concrete steps that led down into the earth. "Stay close."

"No problem there," she said.

He flicked on the flashlight, holding it in front of them as they moved slowly down the steep, narrow stairs. He kept his free hand over one of hers on his waist. The darkness closed in around them. She knew there was light behind her from the cellar, but without turning she couldn't see it. And knowing it was there wasn't nearly reassuring enough. Feeling Jack's warmth suffusing her hand helped more. But it didn't dispel the chill of foreboding that gripped her more thoroughly with every step. It was more than blinding darkness that surrounded her. It was physical, real. It hugged her with cold dampness. She smelled it—

dank and sour. She tasted its bitter, stale, putrid air. She even heard it, containing and muffling every sound.

"God, there's a smell."

"I know."

At the bottom of the stairs, the floor leveled off. Concrete, perfectly rectangular, just tall enough for an adult to walk upright, and only wide enough for one to pass through. Jack's shoulders brushed the walls if he leaned even slightly to one side or the other. It was a concrete tunnel, with only the occasional cobweb blocking the way. And at its end, the darkness widened.

Jack paused, shining the flashlight's beam around. "It's a room, I think." He traced three walls, then examined the fourth, the one with the doorway in which they stood. "I don't see any other exits. This is the only way in."

"Or out," she whispered. "Jack, do you feel that? We're not alone."

He pulled her up beside him, now that there was room to stand two abreast, sliding an arm around her and holding her close as he moved the flashlight beam around the room again, lower this time, tracing the floor from end to end. The light beam stopped when it hit the body.

Kiley yelped and turned her head into Jack's chest. But then she forced herself to look again. Trembling, straining against her own will to turn her head once more, she looked.

The darkly stained bones and leatherlike flesh slumped against the wall. Tangled blond hair clung in patches to the skull.

"There are chains," Jack said. "Look."

She followed the beam of light to the manacles on the wrists and the chains mounted to the walls behind. "This is a nightmare."

"It was for her," Jack said.

And suddenly, the gut-wrenching, bone-numbing fear she had been feeling vanished—replaced by a wave of grief as it hit her that this scary, smelly, partially decomposed body had been a person. A woman, or even a girl. Brought down here, chained up and...

"Oh, God, there are more," Jack said.

She opened her eyes and saw the light moving around the floor, illuminating another corpse, and then another, and another. "Sweet Jesus," she whispered. Tears were welling in her eyes. "It's over, I promise you. God, no wonder you can't rest. No wonder. I promise you, all of this is coming to light. Now."

No.

The word was spoken, she heard it, and yet it felt as if it was not a word at all, but a feeling. A powerful emotion. She heard the trapdoor slam down, behind and above them.

"The spirits of this place aren't ready to let us leave," Jack whispered.

"Maybe they never will be," Kiley said.

Jack touched her shoulders. "Don't think that way."

"How can I not? God, we could be trapped down here. We could die the same horrible way they did." Pulling away from him, she started back along the tunnel, hurrying through the darkness to the stairway, and seeing just what she had expected to see. The closed trapdoor at the top. She went up, pushed at it, but it wouldn't budge.

Jack was behind her, his arms around her, and she turned into them, let him hold her. Eventually she calmed enough to sink onto a step, and he handed her the flashlight and tried to open the door himself, but it was no use.

Sighing, he sank down beside her. "It's going to be all right. Chris knows we're here, he knows we were planning to dig."

"You think anyone will find us if these ghosts don't want them to?"

He sighed. "I think they do want us to be found. Just as they wanted to be found themselves. We just have to wait until they're ready."

"Why the delay? What could they hope to gain?" He pulled her closer, held her beside him. They sat there on the second step from the bottom, the terrible stench of death permeating the air. And slowly, Kiley realized that Jack was shivering. At first it was just a mild ripple, but then it seemed to grow until his entire body vibrated with it. Kiley pulled free of his embrace to look at him. She lifted the flashlight and he shielded his eyes, averted his face.

"What is it. Jack? What's wrong?"

"I don't...know."

Kiley swallowed hard. He'd been shaking earlier, during the seance, too. Just like this. No, not this bad. "What should I do?"

The shaking stopped suddenly, and Jack went very still. His head fell forward, and the rest of his body tried to follow. Kiley gripped his shoulders and kept him from toppling to the floor. She eased him backward instead, lowering his head carefully until it rested on a stair, wishing for a pillow. "Jack? Jack, can you hear me?"

His eyes flashed open then. So suddenly, with such an unnatural look in them that she jerked away from him.

Blinking, calming herself, she leaned closer again. "Jack?"

She was dizzy as she studied his face. He wasn't responding, but at least he'd stopped shaking. God, she had to sit down. She sank onto the step again, let her head fall forward. If she could just rest her eyes for a moment.

But when she lifted her head again she wasn't in the basement anymore. She was upstairs, running herself a hot bath, alone again, and sad at being always so alone.

Her husband was always going on business trips, and he must think she was pretty stupid if he thought she didn't realize something more than business was going on. She felt tears hot on her cheeks and glanced into the mirror.

The face of a beautiful woman looked back at her. Buttery blond hair, piercing, sad eyes. "Phil doesn't love me anymore," Sharon Miller whispered through Kiley's lips. "He never touches me. Something's terribly wrong. There's a coldness in his eyes that wasn't there before."

She turned at the sound of an engine in the driveway. Phil was home early. He would expect her to be asleep, not up weeping. But she had to confront him, now, tonight, before she lost her courage.

She padded downstairs in her nightgown. Only—he didn't come inside. Why wasn't he coming inside?

She moved to the window to peer out at his car in the driveway, and then she noticed that the hatchway door was open. "What is he doing in the cellar?" she asked herself.

Turning from the window, Sharon went down into the basement. There was a trapdoor in the floor. One she had never known was there. Oh, God, she could hear a woman crying. Distant, echoing.

Sharon's heart was beating fast. Somewhere deep inside, Kiley was begging her not to go down there. But she went. Kiley knew she was Kiley, not Sharon, and she knew this was something like being trapped in someone else's nightmare. But she couldn't wake up and she couldn't make it stop.

Turning, she walked the length of the tunnel, ending in the room of horror, where the young wife of long ago had no doubt ended up. And then Kiley saw them, through Sharon's eyes, or was it Sharon reliving it through Kiley's? Women, beautiful young women, chained to the walls. They were dirty, their hair in tangles. They were naked. One hung limply, dead or close to it, but the others were alive and terrified. And her husband, the man she had loved, was forcing the new one to her knees, fastening the chains around her wrists, hitting her when she whimpered and pleaded. "God, what is this?"

Jack—no, not Jack—Phil spun around and saw her there.

"Help us," the girl he'd been chaining up begged. "Please, get out and help us!"

Sharon turned to run, but Phil was too fast for her. He caught her before she made it out, flung her to the floor. She was frightened. God, she had never been si frightened. She couldn't believe this monster was her husband.

He bent over her, clutched her head between his palms. "You have to understand, Sharon. I have needs. Dirty, secret needs. You're too fine a woman for me. I could never use you the way I can them."

"They're girls! They're only girls!"

"Whores. I pick them up in the city, bring them here to satisfy my needs. No one misses them. It's just as well I take them out of the world."

"You...kill them?"

"They don't last well. Get sickly, weak. Eventually they die on their own, or I take mercy on them, put them out of their misery."

She clutched her stomach, doubling over and fighting the urge to vomit. When she got it under control, she tried to straighten again. "How—m-many?" Tears were flowing from her eyes, she could barely see, despite the lights he had strung through the place, trouble lights like they used on construction sites.

He smiled slowly. "Oh, many. Lots and lots of them." He took a breath, sighed. "Come on, my love. I promise, nothing so unpleasant is going to happen to you."

He slid his arm around her shoulders. She shivered, wondering what he would do to her.

"I...won't tell your secret, darling. I would wish things were different. I would ask that you stop this and let them go, but I would never betray you."

"No, of course you wouldn't. Not to your mother, nor to your priest. Good Christian that you are. You'll stay with me, continue loving me, though you think me a rapist and murderer."

The trapdoor was open as he led her up the stairs. Somewhere down deep inside her, Kiley thought that was odd. It had been closed before. Somehow, she was aware that she and Jack were being used as puppets, as the play unfurled again. And she wondered how far it would go.

But then the other one overtook her again. Behind her she could hear the moans and weeping, pleading voices. "Get away from him. Run. Tell someone!"

Ahead of her, she saw light. Her husband yanked a plug from the wall, and the trouble lights went black. The women sobbed, growing hysterical as they were plunged into darkness, but he didn't care. He slammed the steel door down again, never releasing the death grip he had on her arm.

"You're hurting me."

"Not for much longer, love. I promise. Come along now." He took her up the stairs. She felt his grip on her arm relax and she pulled free, racing as fast as she could through the house, toward the door. But he beat her there, blocking her escape. Turning, her heart pounding in her chest, she ran upstairs, seeking the safety of a room with a door she could bolt against him, and a telephone. She went into the bedroom, pushing the door shut.

He slammed into it, but she braced with all her strength, then slid the bolt home. Slowly, she backed away. But he was pounding the door, howling with rage. Bang! Bang! Bang!

"Stay away!" she cried, grabbing the telephone, dialing O.

The door crashed open, and he surged toward her. She heard the line ringing, but he was too close. She dropped the phone, racing into the bathroom and slamming the door.

He kicked it in so fast and hard it hit her full in the chest, knocking her off balance, and she hit the floor. Her head cracked against the porcelain tub. And then it swam. She was dizzy, darkness creeping in around the edges of her vision.

"There, now. You won't die dirty, buried alive, as they do. No, nothing so horrible for my lady." He smiled down at her as he bent over her. "And you've already run the water. That was thoughtful of you." He picked her up, lowered her into the bathtub. His palm to her face, he pushed it beneath the water.

She couldn't breathe! Her arms flailed, legs kicked, but he held firm. And then the water rushed into her lungs. It was gentle, cleansing, soothing. Her body calmed, relaxed. And darkness crept over her.

And then she was standing there, in the bathroom, watching him. He was still leaning over the tub, she realized, puzzled. Then she looked past him and saw her own face in the water.

"He's killed you," a woman said. "He killed us, too." Sharon turned and saw them. Women, beautiful women, all around her. So many faces and sad, sad eyes. "I'm so sorry," she said.

"We have to tell someone. He'll keep on doing it until we stop him."

She nodded and turned to look at her husband again. He was sitting on the floor beside the tub, his head lowered, sobbing.

And then he wasn't her husband, and they weren't in the bathroom. He was Jack McCain, sitting on the bottom steps in the hidden basement bunker, his head in his hands.

Kiley went to him, knelt in front of him. "Jack, it's okay. It's okay, it wasn't real."

He lifted his head slowly, blinked the confusion from his eyes. "Kiley?"

She nodded, and he pressed her face between his palms, pulled her to him, kissed her lips over and over. "You're okay. I thought I—I thought I'd—"

"I'm okay. So are you, and you're not Phillip Miller. You're Jack. All that was—I don't know, it was...it was someone else. It was the past coming in. Sharon Miller reliving it through us, so we'd finally understand."

He nodded, holding her closer.

"It wasn't real. Jack," she told him.

"You're right about everything but that." He brought his head up, looking past her, into the darkness. "It was very real."

She turned to follow his gaze, and she saw them. Faint wisps in the shapes of women. Some were more defined than others, mists shaping into faces and limbs and hands. Others were just vague shapes, silhouettes of light in the darkness. "God, there are so many of them," she whispered. "But there were only four in the room."

Jack rose, clasping her shoulder. "They're buried in the back lawn."

She closed her eyes. "Oh, God."

"It gets worse," he said softly. "He's still doing it."

Her head came up fast. *"What?"*

"Phillip Miller isn't dead, Kiley. He's alive and well and living not far from here. And he's still murdering women." And then she remembered. "The missing prostitutes from Albany. Oh, my God, Jack! We have to get out of here, we have to stop him and—"

There was a groaning sound, and a powerful crash, followed by light spilling in from behind. The trapdoor lay open, the way to the cellar clear.

Kiley met Jack's eyes. "I am so sorry I ever called you a fraud. You're—you're so amazing it's scary."

He shook his head slowly. "Remind me to tell you later why you're dead wrong about that."

She frowned at him. But then she turned to look back at those shapes, the spirits of women, all of them. "It's over. We'll stop him. We promise. And then you can rest in peace."

CHAPTER THIRTEEN

iley's entire house was surrounded in yellow police tape. Police cars, SUVs and vans lined the street, and heavy equipment growled and belched in the back yard. News crews were everywhere, but Kiley wasn't giving any interviews. She'd written what she could about all of this in her latest column, and the rest was going into a book.

She stood on the sidewalk, watching the bodies being exhumed and carried in plastic bags out to waiting vehicles, one after another. Jack sat on the curb close beside her, fallen leaves in brilliant colors carpeting the sidewalk around him, reading the paper.

Officer Hanlon came over to where she stood. "They've arrested Phil Miller. There were three women chained in his basement when they arrived."

Jack looked up from the newspaper. Kiley's throat tightened. "Alive?"

"Yes. Thanks to you."

She swallowed hard. "Thanks for telling me." Hanlon nodded and headed back to the house. Kiley looked down at Jack. "Well?"

He met her eyes, then refocused on the page and began reading aloud from her latest column. "'So to sum it up, I've learned that not everything I don't understand or believe in is necessarily make-believe. There are good psychics and there are bad ones. And the only way to judge which is which is by how they make you feel. If their advice helps you, heals you, answers a need you have, then they are as genuine as any minister, priest, pastor or shrink. I'm retiring from my former career of debunking everything I don't happen to believe in. After what I've seen in my house, I know now that there is far more in this world than I will ever understand. And it humbles me to admit that the extraordinary and genuine skills and gifts of three psychics I called fakes—two of them in this very column—were what enabled me to find the truth about the women who were murdered and buried on my property, and to stop a killer at the end of a thirty-year spree. Those psychics were for real, even though I claimed to have proven otherwise. I will never question what I don't understand again.'"

Jack folded the newspaper and got to his feet. "It's wonderful. Your best column ever."

She shrugged. "If a psychic as gifted as you are doesn't know whether he's a fraud or not, how the hell can I pretend to?" She smiled at him. "I can't believe you were as convinced you were a fake as I was, all this time. How can you have a gift like that and not know?"

Jack shrugged. "Chris knew. He knew all along. I guess it just took a case I cared this much about to make me aware of it."

"Yeah? And what was it about this case that made you care so much?"

He gave her a slow, sexy smile, reached out to clasp her nape and pulled her to him for a long, lingering kiss. His lips moved against hers when he said, "I think you know."

"No way," she whispered back. "You're the one who's psychic, remember?"

"Right. So, I suppose I have to spell it out for you."

She sent him a smile and nodded. "Please."

"I'm nuts about you, Kiley. I don't know when I went from hating you to loving you—maybe it was from the very start. But I know I do."

She nodded. "I was hoping you'd say that."

"Why?"

"Well, I'm going to need a place to crash for a while, for one thing."

He made a face at her. She smiled fully. "And you know, there is that pesky fact that I love you, too."

"Do you?"

"Mmm-hmm."

He kissed her once more, tucked her under his arm and led her back down the sidewalk toward the car. "When the police have finished here, we should have the other psychics in town come back for a cleansing ritual, make sure those spirits have made it across to the other side. They deserve to be at peace," Jack said.

"I agree. But I have a feeling they made it just fine. I feel they're at peace now."

"Yeah, I feel they are, too."

They reached the car, and he opened her door for her. "Where are we going?"

"My place, or I guess I should say our place now."

She shot him a surprised look. "You mean I can move in?"

"Sure you can. Just two things, Kiley."

"What are they?" She got in.

He went around and got behind the wheel. "First, you can't bring any ghosts with you."

"No problem there. And second?"

"Second... is this." He reached past her to open the glove compartment, pulled out a folded sheet of paper and handed it to her.

Frowning, she unfolded it and began to read, then she frowned and looked up at him. "This person thinks he's being haunted."

"Uh-huh. Family curse. Generations. Yada yada."

"Well, that's just...it's ridiculous, Jack."

"Is it, though?"

"You telling me you think it's for real?"

"I do. And since your story hit the news, I've received thirty-seven other letters just like it."

"Thirty-seven–"

"So far." He shrugged. "It felt good, giving those women peace, didn't it? Setting their spirits free. Stopping a killer. Didn't it?"

She thought about it and nodded. "Yeah. It was way more satisfying than debunking frauds ever was."

"So? What do you say?"

"What do I say to what?"

"Working with us. Answering the letters. Investigating, helping where we can."

"We?"

"Chris. Maya. John."

"A whole crew."

"Not whole. Not yet. We need a smartass skeptic to keep us in line, a journalist to document everything, a persistent pain in the ass to help investigate, and a bad ass who's not afraid to yell at ghosts."

"Flattery won't work," she said.

"How about this, then? I need you with me because I can't think straight when you're not. You're on my mind every waking minute. I can't focus on work or much else, to tell you the truth."

They were sitting there, the car running, still parked in the street in front of her house. He was asking her a lot more than just to join his team of ghost hunters, and she knew it.

"That was really good," she said.

"Did it work?"

She looked right into his eyes. "Like a charm."

He kissed her long and slow, then after a deep, satisfied sigh, he pulled the car into motion.

Continue reading for an excerpt from *Cry Wolf*, from the Brown and deLuca Series.

NEW YORK TIMES BESTSELLING AUTHOR

MAGGIE SHAYNE

A Brown and de Luca Novella

CRY WOLF

EXCERPT: CRY WOLF

"*T*his is the first year I've been allowed to come to the fair without grownups," Joshua said. He was walking along the midway, awash in carnival music and the smells of fried foods and horses.

"Are you kidding?" Toby asked. "Man, your family is nuts. I've been coming alone forever. This is like my third year." He ate the last of his cotton candy and tossed the cardboard cone into a nearby wastebasket.

"It's your *second* year," Hunter said. "And you don't come alone, you come with us." Then he shoved the teddy bear he'd just won throwing darts at balloons, into Josh's chest. "Can you fit that in your backpack?"

Toby and Chuckie elbowed each other, grinning.

"It's for my little cousin," Hunter explained as Josh took off his backpack and shoved the purple bear inside. He'd been feeling stupid for bringing one when none of the other guys had. But he'd been carrying their crap around all day, so he guessed it had come in handy. He added the bear to his collection of souvenir slurpy containers, loose change, and Chuck's inhaler.

Josh's best friends were also the three coolest guys in the sixth grade. Seventh grade, once summer vacation was over. Hunter Marks was taller than the others by a solid six inches, and he hadn't been held back even once. He was tougher than any of them. Nobody messed with Hunter, and his basketball skills had earned him the adoration of the entire middle school. Good genes, Josh thought. Toby Gaye took a lot of ribbing for his last name, but he was funny as heck, and that seemed to outweigh it. He was popular by virtue of being the class clown. Chuckie Barnes was the smallest one. He looked like that skinny baby rooster on the cartoons, Foghorn Leghorn's son, right down to the wire-rimmed glasses. His frequent bouts of asthma and scrawny physique would've made him bully bait if he hadn't been part of Hunter and Toby's inner circle.

And now, they'd sort of pulled Josh into their gang. He guessed that made him one of the cool guys now, too. He walked a little taller. After some crazy lady had tried to shoot people at his big brother's graduation party, Josh's popularity among his peers had shot through the roof. And he was glad. His mother being in a nuthouse had been his previous claim to fame. A sniper at a grad party was much cooler. His status, when he entered the seventh grade in a few weeks, was going to be way better than before. And it was about time.

Hitching his backpack up on his shoulders, he nodded toward the scariest ride on the entire midway, the Raptor, and said, "You guys want to go again?"

Each of the guys dug into their pockets to pull out what remained of their ride tickets. Toby had seven, just enough to get on The Raptor one more time. But Hunter was down to two, and Chuck didn't have any.

Josh headed over to the ticket stand, dragged a crumpled twenty-dollar bill out of his pocket, and shoved it through the opening in the plexiglass. A small lady with a chubby hand slid a flat sheet of tickets back out to him, and he started tearing them into strips along the perforations as he rejoined the group, then handed them around.

"Dude, how much money you got on you, anyway?" Hunter asked.

Josh shrugged and Toby said, "Plenty. His parents are like loaded or something. His mom's famous."

"She's not my—I mean, yeah, she *is* kind of famous." They were talking about Rachel, of course, who was not his mother. And Uncle Mason who wasn't his father. But they all lived together, like a real family, so it was close enough. He felt a little guilty about not correcting his friends. But on the other hand, if his friends were starting to forget who his real mother was, then that was a good thing for him, wasn't it?

And his real mom would never know. Right?

The guys took the tickets he gave them. There were three left over, and probably not a ride in the entire park that only took three. Josh looked around, saw a mom with a little kid about four, so he stepped into her path and held them out to her. "You can have these if you want. We're on our last ride for the day anyhow."

She took them and was still looking at him with raised eyebrows when he and the guys walked away to get in line for another round on the Raptor.

"After this, I gotta go," Josh said with a look at his phone. "My brother's picking me up at eight."

"Dude, you could *walk* home from here!" Hunter sounded as if that was a far better option. "Why's he gotta pick you up?"

He was right, of course, but the walk home was two miles over a dirt road that skirted the reservoir on one side and the woods on the other. Seasonal use only. Nobody else on it even in the summer. He hadn't even argued when Uncle Mason had told him that he had to ride home with Jeremy. The idea of walking home that way, after everything that had happened, scared the crap out of him.

Chuck elbowed Hunter. "You've seen his brother's car, though. Who *wouldn't* rather ride in that than walk home?"

The other guys nodded, saving Josh once again from having to explain something that would've been embarrassing. He was still a little bit afraid of the dark, and of long walks on deserted stretches of road in the middle of nowhere. But he didn't want to have to explain all that.

Chuckie grinned at him though, and Josh got the feeling he knew the truth. He smiled back, grateful.

The line moved fast, and the four boys got a car to themselves on one of the four-car pendulums that revolved as they swung higher and higher and higher, maxing out so high they were momentarily suspended upside down and weightless, held in their seats only by the safety bar and each boy's own death grip on it.

It was over way too fast. Josh was proud that he hadn't yelled even once. None of the guys had. But he was a little unsteady on his feet as they got off the ride and headed back onto the midway.

Then he heard a familiar bark—well, you know, the snuffly sound bulldogs call a bark—and looked up to see Myrtle and Hugo galloping toward him. The older blind bulldog, Myrtle, kept her side pressed to the puppy's side the entire way. Hugo was like her seeing-eye pup.

"Aw, dude, cool dogs," Hunter said when Myrtle bashed her iron skull into Josh's shin.

Josh crouched down, petting them both. "Hey, Myrtle, meet the guys. Guys, this is Myrtle. She's blind but she gets around great. And the pup is Hugo."

The guys bent to pet the dogs, too, and Jeremy, who was right behind the dogs, said, "Hey guys. Good day?"

They all straightened, maybe standing a little taller in the presence of Josh's big brother, Jeremy, who was far cooler than any of them by virtue of his advanced age, recent graduation, and classic ride.

"The best," Toby said.

"It was all right," Hunter said at the same time.

Chuckie stayed crouched, petting the dogs, talking to them like they were people.

"Any of you guys need a ride home?" Jeremy asked.

"We brought our bikes," Hunter said.

"Okay, that's cool. You ready, Josh?"

"Yep. See you guys. C'mon, Myrt."

Myrt abandoned Hugo to press herself against Josh's leg and they wound their way back to the parking lot and climbed into Jeremy's Iroc Z. Jere revved the motor a little, showing off for the guys while he waited for traffic to clear so he could pull out and to the left. A quarter mile later, he took a right at the stoplight, and kept going until the pavement ended, and the woods began on the left, the reservoir's sloping shore on the right.

Two miles up on the left was where they lived in a giant camper with Aunt Rachel and Uncle Mason. His friends were right about Rachel. She was loaded, and so after the firebug had torched her house, she'd picked out the biggest, fanciest camper he'd ever seen. It had four slide-out sections, a satellite dish, three TVs, and a patio. It sat on the front lawn about fifty yards from the house, which was in the process of being rebuilt.

It was pretty cool how they'd all sat down together, throwing out ideas while Uncle Mason sketched pictures and Aunt Rachel took notes. She said this time, the house was gonna be *their* dream home, not just hers, because they were all living there together from now on.

He guessed that meant she and Uncle Mace were official. And he was glad.

Josh's room was gonna be a gamer's paradise. Jeremy was getting an apartment over the garage, so he would have his own space during breaks from college, which started in just a couple of weeks. Right now their dream house was just a big empty shell, but they'd only been working on it just over a month.

It was August 1st, and life was changing. Life had been changing for him and Jeremy for a couple of years now, but this time, he thought it was changing into something really awesome. And it was about time, too.

Jere parked the car near the camper and cut the motor. Josh opened his door, and the puppy dove out of the car and stood on the ground barking like mad. Josh helped Myrtle out, picking her right up and then setting her on the ground. "Jere, I think she's getting lighter." Then he frowned. "And look, her neck rolls aren't covering up her collar anymore."

"Shh. Don't let Rachel hear you say that or—"

"Don't let Rachel hear you say what?" Rachel said, coming out the camper's little door and dropping into a crouch as Myrtle raced toward her. She caught the dog's face in her hands before she got her shins bashed. Good trick, Josh thought.

"That Myrtle's losing some of her chub," he told her. "I guess the Dr. Clive was right." Josh noticed Jeremy wincing and closing his eyes.

Rachel frowned. "Dr. Clive was *not* right," she said. "Myrtle isn't losing weight. She's in perfect shape, and has been all along. Cutting out the tiny little tastes we feed her from our dinner plates—"

"And lunch plates," Jeremy said, "and breakfast plates, and bedtime snacks, and cheese sticks. Don't forget the cheese sticks."

"—hasn't made one bit of difference," Rachel continued, after sending Jeremy a lovingly withering glare. "Because we haven't been giving her enough to *make* a difference. She wasn't over-weight. That vet is full of shi...blue mud."

"Right. I hear a lot of Cornell-educated vets are," Jeremy added a smile, then before Rachel could respond, said, "Yo, Josh, get your crap outta my car, huh?"

Josh turned back toward the car, but Rachel was still talking. "Myrtle is just the right size for a big-boned bulldog," she said, rubbing Myrt's ears just the way she liked best. "Aren't you, Myrt? Yes, you are."

The bulldog wiggled her butt, because she didn't have a tail. Just a curly little stub on her backside. Although, Josh thought that curly stub was protruding from her rump more than before. Yeah, she had definitely lost weight.

He reached into Jeremy's car, picked his backpack up from the seat, and then said, "Aw, crap!" Rachel and Jeremy both turned his way, waiting for the rest.

"I forgot, I've got all the guys' stuff in my backpack."

"Anything that can't wait until tomorrow?" Rachel asked. Josh pulled out Chuckie's inhaler, held it up, and she said, "Nope, guess not."

"I'll take him, Aunt Rache," Jeremy offered. "If we hurry, we can catch them before they even get home."

"Thanks Jeremy." Rachel clasped her hands near her chin and batted her eyes. "You're so selfless."

"Yeah, and you love driving your car anywhere for any reason," Josh added.

"You reap most of the benefits of that, squirt. Hop in."

"Make it quick," Rachel said. "And by quick, I mean keeping to the speed limit, Jere. You know, within reason."

He sent her a nod and got behind the wheel. Josh buckled up, and the car headed right back the way it had come from, rumbling and growling to the end of their road and then left through the village.

"So who lives closest?" Jere asked.

"Hunter. The next road on the right." The other guys lived farther along the main drag, Chuckie on the left, and Toby a little farther, on a dirt side road not unlike Josh's own.

Jeremy turned onto Hunter's road. "How far up?"

"Not far. Top of the hill and then around a sharp curve, and then—wait, wait. Jeremy stop!"

Jere hit the brakes right in the middle of the road and sent

Josh his patented WTF look, but Josh was already trying to open the door, and then he finally did and got out and ran to the bike he'd spotted lying on its side in the ditch. He scrambled down to it, his feet splashing into the water that ran in the bottom. "It's Hunter's bike!"

"Holy crap." Jeremy was out of the car, too, looking left and right, and shouting, "Hunter! Hunter, where the heck are you?"

Josh started to reach for the bike to pull it out of the mud, but he stopped when he saw what looked like blood on the handlebar. "Jere?"

His big bro was right behind him by then. "Don't touch it, Josh. He probably tried some BMX move or something and crashed. Probably limped home for a Band-Aid." He was pulling out his phone, and a second later, said, "What's his number?"

"I have it on my phone." Josh was trembling as he pulled his phone out of his pocket, scrolled to Hunter's entry and tapped the button to call his landline. The water was starting to seep into his sneakers. Mrs. Marks picked up on the second ring.

"Just ask if he's there," Jere whispered. "Don't scare her. We don't know if there's a reason to yet."

Nodding in a jerky motion, Josh said, "Hey, Miz Marks, it's Josh. Is Hunter home?"

"No, but I expect him soon. I told him before dark, so he should be here any minute. Weren't you at the fair with him?"

"Uh, yeah, but I went home and realized he left some stuff in my backpack."

"Oh, well, did you try texting him?"

"I didn't uh…didn't think of that. Thanks, Miz Marks." He ended the call, and looked up at Jeremy, who was already making a call of his own, and Josh hoped it was to Uncle Mason. Jere put his phone on speaker, and held it between the two of them.

While it rang, Jere said, "Hunter's probably still walking. Maybe he crashed his bike within the last few minutes, and he just hasn't made it home yet."

"It's not that far," Josh said, looking up the hill. He could see the beginning of the curve. Hunter's house was just the other side of it.

"Hey, Jere, what's up?" Uncle Mason's voice came from the phone speaker. Just hearing it made Josh feel a little better.

Jere nodded at him, a sort of it's-gonna-be-okay kind of nod, and said, "Hey, Uncle Mace. Um, Josh's friend Hunter was riding his bike home from the fair, last we knew. But we just found his bike in a ditch down the road from his house, and his mom says he's not home yet."

"Where's Josh? Are you safe?"

"I'm right here, Uncle Mace. We're fine."

"We're by the bike now," Jeremy said. "Right where we found it."

"Okay, stay there for now, but get in the car and lock it. Don't touch the bike. Does Hunter have a cell?" Uncle Mason asked.

"Just an iPod, but he can text with it," Josh said. "Uncle Mason, there's blood on the handlebar." He hated how hard his voice was shaking.

"I'm on my way, Josh. I'm gonna be right there. Five minutes. Get in the car and lock it, just to be on the safe side. Anyone besides me shows up, you just drive away, okay?"

"We'll drive up and down the road," Jeremy said. "See if we spot him walking or..." He shot a quick look at Josh. "...or anything."

"Okay. Do that. I'll be there soon."

Jeremy pocketed his phone and said, "Come on, let's get back in the car, kiddo."

But Josh had turned to look back at the bike in the ditch and kind of got stuck there. He couldn't even blink. "It's like we're contagious," he said.

"What do you mean?" Standing right behind him, Jeremy dropped his hand on Josh's shoulder. He had big hands all of the sudden, Josh realized. His hands were grown-up hands. When had that happened?

"It's like we've got some kind of curse on us or something, and now it's spreading to our friends. I've only been hanging out with Hunter for a month, and it's already got him."

"Aw come on, Josh." Jere tugged on his shoulder until he turned Josh around. "You know there's no curse. We've had some bad luck, that's all. This is probably nothing. Hunter's probably fine, prob'ly knocked a tooth out on his handlebar and ran home crying."

"Not Hunter. Hunter doesn't cry." Josh looked up at his brother and said, "Something bad happened to him, Jere. I feel it, right here." He pressed a fist into his belly and tried to keep breathing past the knot in his throat. "And I don't know how, but I think it's because of us."

"Shoot, you're starting to act like you're the one with NFP."

His reference to Aunt Rachel's gift, which she called NFP for not effing psychic, made Josh smile, and his heart felt a little bit lighter.

Cry Wolf is now available!

ABOUT THE AUTHOR

New York Times bestselling author Maggie Shayne has published more than 50 novels and 23 novellas. She has written for 7 publishers and 2 soap operas, has racked up 15 Rita Award nominations and actually, finally, won the damn thing in 2005.

Maggie lives in a beautiful, century old, happily haunted farmhouse named "Serenity" in the wildest wilds of Cortland County, NY, with her soul-mate, Lance. They share a pair of English Mastiffs, Dozer & Daisy, and a little English Bulldog, Niblet, and the wise guardian and guru of them all, the feline Glory, who keeps the dogs firmly in their places. Maggie's a Wiccan high priestess (legal clergy even) and an avid follower of the Law of Attraction.

Find Maggie at http://maggieshayne.com

f facebook.com/maggieshayneauthor
🐦 twitter.com#!/maggieshayne
📷 instagram.com/maggieshayne
BB bookbub.com/authors/maggie-shayne

ALSO BY MAGGIE SHAYNE